PENGUIN BOOKS

Heartbreak High

Heartbreak High

Rap Pack

Meredith Costain

PENGUIN BOOKS

PENGUIN BOOKS

Published by the Penguin Group
Penguin Books Ltd, 27 Wrights Lane, London W8 5TZ, England
Penguin Books USA Inc., 375 Hudson Street, New York, New York 10014, USA
Penguin Books Australia Ltd, Ringwood, Victoria, Australia
Penguin Books Canada Ltd, 10 Alcorn Avenue, Toronto, Ontario, Canada M4V 3B2
Penguin Books (NZ) Ltd, 182–190 Wairau Road, Auckland 10, New Zealand

Penguin Books Ltd, Registered Offices: Harmondsworth, Middlesex, England

First published in Australia by Penguin Books Ltd 1994
First published in Great Britain in Penguin Books 1994
1 3 5 7 9 10 8 6 4 2

Printed in England by Clays Ltd, St Ives plc

Chapter One

'Nick! Hurry up! Con is waiting!'

Let him wait, thought Nick. *Today, I have to look good. The best!*

Nick cranked the volume up another notch on his tape player, and sang along with the Chili Peppers. He checked himself out in the mirror. Man, what a body. Those pecs! That profile!

Maybe just a little more after-shave. There. Now for the hair. It was so thick, he could never get it to sit just how he wanted it. Mmm. Not bad. Looking pretty good. After all, it *was* the first day back at school. He just *had* to make a good first impression on any new babes that might happen to show up.

'Nick! Your sister's got school too, you know!

It was his mother again. Well, his sister could wait. They could all wait. Nick Poulos would come out when he was good and ready. He reached for the comb again.

In the kitchen, his cousin Con was getting edgy. He hated waiting around for anyone, specially when there were deals lined up, just begging to be made.

'Hurry up, man!' he called. 'We've got twenty minutes!'

Nick wiped a stray blob of shaving cream from his cheek. 'Quit hassling. I'm coming!' he called back.

'When, this year?' groaned Con, pushing back the mop of glistening brown curls threatening to invade his eyes. Effie, Nick's little sister, offered to lend him a scrunchie.

Nick's mother shrugged her shoulders. She was used to this. 'He spends more time in the bathroom than his sister. You want two pieces of toast, Con?'

'One's fine, thanks, Aunty Ireni. With jam.' He reached for the coffee pot and poured two cups, one for Nick's father who had pulled up a chair at the table, just back from night shift at the factory. 'How's it going, Uncle George?'

'Good, Con, good.' He rubbed his eyes and gestured towards the bathroom. 'Is Nick *still* in there?'

Effie nodded. 'He's hopeless.'

'Slow motion. That's what he is in the morning.' He gently waved his arms and legs around, slow motion style, making Effie giggle. 'He needs a fast motion kick up the backside!'

'Hey!' called Nick from the bathroom. 'I heard that!'

Con laughed, then made a dive for his bag. His mobile phone was ringing.

'You're such a poser, Con,' said Effie, taking her dishes to the sink.

Con gave her the finger. But nicely. She *was* his favourite cousin. 'Plaka Auto Parts? Right, no worries.' He telescoped the aerial and put the phone back in his bag. 'Wrong number.'

His uncle shook his head. Kids today!

'Well, what do you reckon?' Nick stood framed in the bathroom doorway, wearing 501s, a white Hanes, and Raybans. He looked ready for a night on the town rather than a day in the classroom.

2

His father shook his head. 'I think a couple of years in the army – the discipline, the simple life – would do you – and you particularly, Con – a lot of good. Now get out of here, both of you.'

Nick laughed and swiped the piece of toast his father had just finished buttering from under his nose. He nodded at Con. 'What are you waiting for? We're out of here!'

Hartley Road, at eight-thirty in the morning, was hot and hazy. Semi-trailers and commuters' cars battled for space on the narrow roads. The pavements were already beginning to fill up as shoppers, representing most nations in the world, took advantage of the array of ethnic goodies to be found in the local shopping centre.

Con swung his pride and joy – a '63 black open-top Buick – out into the peak-hour traffic, speakers blaring INXS, on the lookout for Steve and Danielle. He spotted them outside the Lebanese deli, snogging as usual. It was like they were joined at the lips or something.

He pulled up beside them and bleeped the horn. 'Hey, you guys, if I'm not interrupting . . .'

'Con! Nick! How's it going, mate?' Danielle slid her long, tanned legs into the back seat of the Buick, dragging Steve in beside her.

The car lurched off with a squeal of tyres. Moments later it had jerked to a stop again – this time at a red light. To their left, ensconced in a red, late model hatchback, a young blonde woman was studying a street directory, a frown pulling at her pretty face.

Nick spotted her first. He dropped his shades to get a better look, then turned to grin at Con. 'I'm in love, man!'

He leaned over towards the blonde, giving her the benefit of his most wicked smile. 'Where you going? You need some directions?'

The blonde tried to ignore him, but failed miserably. Nick tended to have that effect on people. All kinds of people.

'My name's Nick. What's yours?' Still no response. Oh well. He'd just have to try harder. Steve and Con were hollering beside him, blowing kisses. No style.

'Don't listen to them. Me, I'm a nice guy. So, what are we doing tonight, uh?'

The lack of response didn't faze him. 'You gonna give me your phone number? Come on, give us the last three digits then. Your postcode? You gotta give me something!'

Con revved the Buick. 'She's not interested, Nick. Wave goodbye to the lady.'

'Hey, I'm in love with this woman. She's beautiful!'

He turned to blow kisses at her from their rapidly departing car. 'Bye, beautiful!' he called. How had he let that one get away?

Jack Nguyen headed off to the bus stop on the corner, his new schoolbag hanging from one shoulder. He managed to ignore a couple of Grammar School boys in the bus queue, all decked out in stripy blazers, caps and ties. They looked him up and down, pointing out his lack of uniform, and cracking jokes about his 'slanty' eyes. What was harder to deal with was the old man who moved to another seat when Jack sat down beside him. He'd muttered something about how the Japanese were taking over the country these days. Couldn't he even tell the difference between a Japanese and a Vietnamese person? Or maybe, thought Jack, he just didn't care. Lots of people were like that. If you were Asian, or even looked slightly Asian, you were all lumped together.

The bus wound through the inner-city streets, dropping off passengers here and there. Eventually it arrived at his destination: Hartley High. Jack followed a group of kids down the steps of the bus and out onto the footpath, then, after stopping briefly to ask directions, walked calmly into the administration building.

'Place hasn't changed much, that's for sure.' Danielle unwound herself from Steve and climbed out of the back seat. 'Same old faces.'

'Maybe there'll be some new teachers to stir,' said Con, checking out the schoolground. It was hardly a palace – in fact it could almost be mistaken for a prison. A double-storey brick building dominated the yard, which was paved with gritty, knee-gouging asphalt. The grounds were separated from the street by a high cyclone wire fence; there wasn't a tree or a stick of greenery to be seen. Some well meaning art teacher had attempted to brighten up the surroundings by getting her Year 10 class to paint a couple of murals on the walls one year, but they were the only bright flashes of colour in an otherwise grey environment. This was the inner suburbs, all right.

Con looked around for the rest of their gang. Kids, their clothes ranging from Westie-style check shirts and hooded sweats to skater-style T-shirts and baggy shorts, were sitting around in small groups, catching up on six weeks of holiday gossip, or kicking balls around the asphalt. He watched as a small, shiny red hatchback pulled neatly into the teachers' parking lot. He grabbed Nick's arm excitedly. 'Hey man, look who it is!'

Nick swivelled round. It was the blonde!

He ambled over, oozing macho charm. 'You followed us here, didn't you!'

The blonde regarded him coolly. She looked far too young to be a teacher, and her outfit – jeans and a sleeveless shirt – wasn't much different from the clothes worn by half the students in the yard. It was the shiny new briefcase and pile of text books she was holding that gave her away.

Nick grinned. He had the situation sussed now. 'Are you a teacher, Miss?'

'Yeah', she said, giving a little crooked smile as she walked past. 'I am'.

'I still want your phone number,' called Nick.

Con did a double take. This babe was a teacher? Oh well. That meant she was fair game. 'Welcome to hell, teacher,' he called. He watched her walk unsteadily through the milling groups of kids. This one was as green as they came. He'd give her two weeks. Tops.

Steve had noticed her shakiness too. He could almost smell the fear. He leaned in close to her. 'Hey, Miss. What do you teach?'

She stopped for a moment, studying the cheeky, round face only inches from hers. 'English and er . . . history.'

'So, are you going to teach me?' breathed Steve, popping his blue eyes at her.

Danielle had had enough. She punched Steve on the arm. Hard. He withdrew to the sidelines.

Another face loomed out of the crowd gathering around the new teacher. Rivers. This guy was trouble with a capital T. He'd only been at the school two years, but he'd already managed to carve out a reputation for himself as a bully. He

6

was a big guy, and used his height and build to his advantage. Danielle winced, knowing what was coming.

He clamped his baseball cap down more firmly over his long, straggling curls. 'You give special classes after school, Miss?' he asked silkily. His mates elbowed each other. Rivers. What a legend!

But he'd met his match. The rookie teacher squared her shoulders and looked him straight in the eye.

'I do, in fact,' she said, simply. 'Detention.'

'Good one,' thought Danielle, as she watched the teacher disappear into the relative safety of the staffroom. Maybe this one wasn't so green after all!

'To me! To me! Pass it to me!'

The teachers had disappeared into the caverns of the staff-room to do whatever teachers do on the first day back, leaving the students to their own devices. Which, for Nick and the gang, meant an impromptu soccer game in the yard.

Danielle had control of the ball. She weaved through several players, looking for an opening, then expertly kicked it to Nick, who tried to pass it on to Con. Except he'd judged it badly. The ball flew past Con and bounced near a group of kids watching the game. Nick watched as one of them, a tall, slim Vietnamese guy, trapped the ball with his chest, then neatly kicked it back into play.

Nick was impressed. 'Hey, good pass, man,' he said, taking some time to check out the neatly dressed guy standing on the sidelines. Unlike the rest of the students, who stood gathered together in little friendship groups, this guy was alone. He hadn't seen him around before. 'What's your name?'

7

The guy answered non-committally, his face a mask. 'Jack. I'm new.'

Nick was taken aback. He'd only been trying to be friendly! But he didn't have time to sort out this guy's problems – the ball was heading his way again. He decided to give this Jack guy the benefit of the doubt; maybe he was just shy, being new and all. 'I'm Nick!' he called, heading off down the other end of the yard in pursuit of the ball. 'Wanna play soccer?'

It was enough. Jack put his bag down, and joined the group, passing the ball like he'd been playing with these kids all his life. Danielle smiled. This guy was good! They could do with some new talent.

She trapped the ball and sent it whizzing past Rivers' nose to Jack. Rivers looked up, annoyed. *Jerk*, she thought. Now there was a guy with a definite *lack* of talent.

Rivers stopped eating his cake long enough to check out the match in progress. He noticed the new player, and didn't like what he saw.

'Hey fellas,' he said to his mates, 'check it out. Looks like the wog ball team's got a new recruit.' He stood up, making sure his next jibe would be heard by his target. 'Thought slopes only played ping-pong!' he jeered.

Danielle gasped and looked quickly at Jack. If the remark had upset him he showed no sign of it. He played stolidly on. 'Go stick your head under a bus!' called back Danielle. Rivers made her sick.

'If I had a head like yours, Danielle darling, I would,' he taunted.

Right. That was it. She started to move towards him, eyes flashing. But Nick was quicker off the mark. And ultimately more successful.

8

'Danielle,' he called. 'Watch this!'

It was beautiful. A perfect kick sent the ball arcing through the air, to connect up with Rivers' piece of chocolate cake, knocking it out of his hand.

Jack laughed, and picked up the ball. It was a big mistake. Rivers pounced on him.

'What are you laughing at, socket-head?'

Jack shrugged. He'd heard it all before. 'Nothing.'

Rivers tapped two fingers on Jack's chest, his face menacing. 'Give me the ball, wimp.'

Nick and Con appeared behind him, begging Jack to kick the ball to them. Rivers kept up his barrage. 'Come on you gutless slope, give me the ball.'

Jack looked straight ahead. There was no way he wanted a fight, not on his first day. Not over this. He handed the ball to Rivers and walked silently away.

Nick couldn't believe it. 'What are you doing, man?'

Jack kept walking. 'It's not my fight,' he said softly.

Nick watched him walk away. That had taken guts, playing it cool like that. Maybe there was more to this new kid than met the eye. And he was right. It wasn't his fight. It was their fight. His and Con's and Zlatco's and all the gang that Rivers loved to hate. All the wogs who loved to play the 'wog game' – soccer. Meanwhile, there was still the problem of the ball to deal with. Rivers still had it. A very angry Rivers.

Rivers stood in front of Nick, brandishing the ball. 'Look what I've got,' he taunted.

Nick snapped. 'What are you trying to pull?'

'Your chain, greaseball!' Rivers danced around him, twirling on his toes. 'Ay ay. I'm a Greek. Hey Conny boy! My beautiful little boosdi boy. You scored me a goal. Gimme a kiss.'

He smacked his lips, making kissing sounds. 'You bunch of fairies,' he said in disgust.

It was enough for Nick. He lunged at Rivers, knocking the ball out of his hands. Rivers pushed him back. Within moments most of the rest of the kids in the schoolyard had joined in, girls and guys, lashing out at any spare parts of enemy flesh they could get their hands on, or barracking from the sidelines.

A blind in the staff-room flew up, revealing a knot of teachers looking on with resigned expressions. So the kids were fighting already, were they? So what else was new. It was just another day at Hartley High.

The bell rang, signalling the start of class. Kids picked themselves up from the asphalt, dusted themselves down, and filed into the building. Nick and Con were happy; they were in the same home-group together yet again. Eleven B. 'B for brains, mate,' said Con, giving Nick a push.

'B for beautiful,' said Nick, checking out the girl heading up the corridor towards them. This one had style. Blonde hair, big, kohl-lined eyes, essential features in all the right places. And her clothes! A strappy little singlet revealing a lacy black bra, masses of jewellery, curve-hugging jeans. Nobody at Hartley High came to school dressed like that. Nobody!

He watched her peer at the numbers on the lockers, then turn a key and open the one next to his. It must be fate. He straightened his T-shirt and ran his fingers through his dark, wavy hair before introducing himself.

'How you going? I'm Nick. Need anyone to show you around?'

The girl studied his face for a minute with a look that would make slaters curl up and die, then turned back to her locker.

'No,' she said, flipping through her books as though they were the most interesting things she'd seen all day.

Nick tried another tack. 'You in my class?'

'I hope not.'

What was with this girl? Normally he had to fight them off! 'I'm Nick Poulos.'

Jodie yawned. 'Good for you.' She checked her time-table and sauntered off.

'Did you see that?' said Nick, scratching his head. Chicks today! What was with them? Con laughed, and pulled him down the corridor. 'Don't worry, mate,' he said, watching the vision walk into Room 27, 'you'll get another chance. Looks like we're all in the same class this year.'

Nick looked down at his time-table. First up – Room 27. English with Ms Milano. He watched the small, blonde teacher they'd hassled in the schoolground that morning walk uncertainly in and set up her desk. Two gorgeous new women in the one day! It certainly *was* going to be an interesting year!

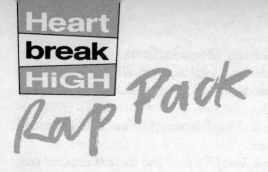

Chapter Two

Nick watched the new teacher nervously trying to control the class. She was hopeless – had no idea at all. It was the same every year. New teachers, fresh out of college, thrown like lambs to the slaughter. Teaching. What a loser job!

Nick looked around the classroom at the grimy walls, shoe-scuffed floor and graffiti-covered plastic chairs. 'Wogs suck!' was scrawled in letters twenty centimetres high on the blackboard. The place was a dump. He couldn't imagine why anyone would want to work here, or in any school for that matter. Even the corridors smelled like mouldy socks and soggy banana sandwiches, and it was only the first day back! Nick had definite ideas about what he wanted to get out of school. A good laugh with his mates, and plenty of soccer at lunchtime.

His father, like the good Greek father that he was, was always going on at him about how important school was – how you needed an education if you wanted to get a good job. Nick's grandparents had migrated to Australia in the 1950s, when his father had only been a baby, hoping to secure a better future for their children than what was on offer in war-torn Europe.

It hadn't made much difference – his father had ended up on the assembly line of a local car manufacturing plant. But he still had big dreams for his own children.

But Nick didn't need a job, did he. As far as he was concerned, his future was all mapped out. Education would play little part in it. He was going to play professional soccer.

He watched Rivers and Bolton give the teacher major grief. All she was trying to do was get everyone sitting down, but they were turning the whole thing into World War Three.

'What's your name, Miss?' called Bolton, wandering out to the front of the room. Bolton was Rivers' best mate. With his shaved head and steel-capped, bovver-boy boots, he looked like a fully fledged member of the Neo-Nazi brigade.

'Sit in your seat, please,' answered the teacher, through gritted teeth.

Rivers snorted. 'Miss Sit-In-Your-Seat-Please. That's a funny name.'

The rest of the class broke up. The teacher turned to the board, and ignoring the squeaking chalk that broke half-way through, carefully wrote her name – Ms Milano.

'Miss Mil-ano,' chanted the class, like first-graders. 'Good mor-ning Miss Mil-ano.'

The teacher smiled shyly, and peering at the roll, began to call out the names. Her tongue stumbled over unfamiliar sounds: 'Anastasia Anathasolopoulos... Agape Babatzikos... Jim Bolton... Con Bordino... Truc Diem...'

The class broke up. She'd pronounced Truc 'truck.' Bolton made brrrrrmmming noises. 'It's pronounced 'trook', Miss,' offered Danielle, helpfully.

'Yeah, rhymes with gook,' squealed Rivers. Jack stiffened in his chair, then shot a cold look at them.

13

'Quiet!' yelled the teacher. The knuckles on the hand holding the chalk were white.

A phone trilled. Con immediately dove for cover under his desk, and began furiously selling car parts. Nick smiled. Con always put his business interests first, no matter *where* he was.

He sneaked a look over at the new girl. Her name was Jodie, according to Ms Milano's roll. Jodie. Now there was a name he could grow to love.

Nick had never really had any problems getting girlfriends. He was popular with his mates, funny, and ... not that he'd ever admit it himself ... serious spunk material. Last Year he'd had three Year 9 girls clamouring for his attentions. One of them had even spent two whole weekends hanging around outside his house, hoping to catch a glimpse of him. His sister Effie had told him about it, and he'd been really embarrassed. And he'd broken another girl's heart when he passed up her offer to go skating one Saturday, preferring to watch his soccer team, Sydney Olympic, with Con and Danielle and the rest of the gang.

But this new chick. Jodie. She wasn't like anyone he'd ever met before. He wondered what sort of things she liked, what stuff she was into. Maybe, if he could find that out, he could get talking some time, suggest a little outing, just for the two of them. He left the initiation of the new teacher to the experts, and settled into a daydream ...

Forty minutes later he was back out in the schoolyard, bouncing a soccer ball on his knees. When Jodie walked past on her way to the toilets, he bounced up to her instead.

'Hey ... how's it going?'

Jodie sniffed. 'All right till you came along.'

Nick's confidence took a knock, but only for a moment.

Well, at least she was talking to him! He pirouetted, flipped the ball off his feet and onto his head and turned back to check her reaction.

'See you round, uh?' He ambled off in the opposite direction. Mr Cool. That was the style he normally adopted for winning hearts. He could see no reason to change it ... yet.

Jodie raised an eyebrow. 'Like a performing seal, isn't he?' she said, to no one in particular.

Nick was feeling a little guilty. They'd just had their second class for the day with Ms Milano, and this time the guys had really turned it on. He'd been right in there with the rest of them. Well, teacher-baiting was a national sport, wasn't it? Anyway, Jodie hadn't been in the class to occupy his mind. A man had to do something to pass the time, right?

The rookie teacher had flipped, basically. She'd screamed something at them about behaving like animals - well, Con *was* giving his best gorilla impression at the time - and then done the big walk-out scene on them. Probably hiding out in the toilets, he guessed. That's where they all ended up, he reckoned, standing in front of the mirror, reflecting on their misfortune to be posted to 'Heartbreak High.'

That had left them with half a lesson and nothing to do. Time was too precious to be wasted hanging around a classroom. Rivers had led them over the wall - or out the window in this case. Half the class would have disappeared down the back of the oval or over to the cafe by now.

But not him. He had more important business to attend to. Playing it cool with Jodie hadn't exactly paid off. It was time for some affirmative action.

Nick pulled a rubbish bin over to the science-room window,

upended it, and stood on the top to get a better view. Aah. There she was, up near the front.

'Pssssttttt.'

Jodie didn't move. Come on, thought Nick, she must have heard that.

After waiting for the chemistry teacher to turn his back to the class, he ripped a piece of paper out of a new folder, scrawled a note on it, and hastily folded it into a paper plane. Blowing a kiss towards the back of Jodie's head, he launched the plane, then raised his fist in triumph when he saw it slide effortlessly onto the desk in front of her. 'Yes!'

Jodie looked up, surprised, to see a face frantically blowing kisses at her from the window. Reaching disdainfully for the plane, she screwed it up, and made a great show of flicking it into the bin.

The next time she looked up, the face in the window was gone. It reappeared a moment later, this time with a yellow daisy in its teeth. Nick then launched into full-on Romeo mode, clutching his heart, mopping his brow ...

The room erupted into giggles. The teacher, Mr Southgate, interrupted his talk on natural disasters and came over to see what all the fuss was about.

As if on cue, Nick disappeared from sight.

'There's one outside the window, sir,' said Jodie primly.

Southgate froze. 'I beg your pardon?'

'A natural disaster, sir. Outside the window.'

Unfortunately, just as Southgate reached the window, Nick appeared yet again, flower and all, intent on capturing his prize.

Southgate calmly eyeballed him. 'I'd say disaster's an understatement,' he purred. 'Catastrophe's probably more appropriate

16

in this case.' He snatched the wilting flower from Nick's mouth, depositing it on Jodie's desk on his way back to the front of the room. The class sighed at the romance of it all.

'Go on, you stupid goat, get back to class!'

Nick did a disappearing act. Jodie turned back to her chemistry book, a smile playing about her lips. So the 'goat' was smitten, eh? Well, he'd keep. He wasn't really her style, anyway. Too much 'one of the boys'. Definite dork material. Picking up her pen, she started work on the first problem, hoping it wasn't going to prove too difficult to solve.

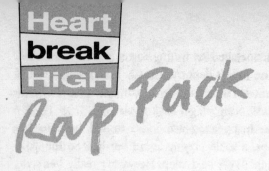

Chapter Three

Jack looked at his watch. 8.20. The schoolground was pretty deserted at this hour. He'd have time to get to the library and put in some extra study before classes started. He dropped his bag on the ground outside the toilets and headed inside, thinking about the day ahead of him. It would be a relief to have some time to himself at school. Every time he turned around it seemed like Rivers and his mates were on his back, taunting and goading him. Making personal comments about his eyes and skin colour. Or just telling him to 'go home'.

They'd been at it again yesterday, in Ms Milano's class, where the class had been asked to fill out job information selection sheets. Most of them had treated it as a big joke, putting down things like aerobics instructor. But for him, the whole thing had been deadly serious.

He wanted to be a doctor.

Until yesterday, no-one else had known about it, outside his family. Not the teachers, not anyone. It was his own special dream. One that he knew he could achieve if he worked hard enough.

That jerk Rivers had laughed in his face when he'd confessed

18

his ambitions in class. And he'd gone on and on about how the newcomers to the country had taken all the jobs. But it just wasn't true! There were many, many people in his community who hadn't been able to get a job at all. Look at his own father! In Vietnam, he'd been a doctor. But here – in Australia, the great 'lucky country' as everyone kept calling it – he'd been lucky to get a job as a cleaner.

Jack thought back to the hardships his family had faced over the years. Kids in Australia had it so easy – if only they knew what living in a country like Vietnam could be like. The war that had started long before he was even born had destroyed his beautiful country and the lives of many of the people who lived in it. When his family decided to leave, he'd experienced mixed feelings. Sadness at having to leave his cousins and grandparents behind, but an eagerness to begin life in a new country, free of a tyrannical regime.

His family – his mother, father, sister Thuy and brother Duc – after much scrimping and saving, had managed to secure passage on a small boat, bound for Indonesia. It had taken ages to get to the port of Vung Tau, and when they finally arrived, his brother had wandered off to the markets, searching for some extra provisions to take on the journey. It was then that the greatest tragedy of his life had struck. The sailors, eager to start the trip, had herded the waiting passengers on board, deaf to the protests of his parents that their eldest son was missing. The boat had sailed, his mother and sister screaming at the sailors to wait for just ten ... just five more minutes ....

He'd never seen his brother Duc again.

It had taken another two years to finally reach Australia. The boat trip had been horrendous. Seventy-five people had been crammed onto a tiny deck so closely that there hadn't even been room to lie down. For the first few weeks, they'd survived on a meagre diet of rice and dried, fried fish. Their daily water ration would only have filled one of the test-tubes in the chemistry lab. When their supplies finally ran out, they'd floated for three days on stormy seas without food or water, frozen, hungry and cramped.

A fishing boat, full of friendly faces from Singapore, had rescued them when all hope seemed lost. The fishermen had fed Jack and his family, then set their boat on the right course for Indonesia. They'd lived for a time on Pulau Galang, a beautiful island off the coast of Indonesia, but eventually travelled on by boat to Singapore, then plane to Sydney. After a year in a hostel, they'd moved around a lot, trying to find somewhere to live where they felt accepted and welcome.

And now Jack was here, in Hartley. A new suburb; a new school. A new set of problems to deal with.

It had taken all of his will-power to stop himself from physically attacking Rivers when, looking for an easy target, he'd insulted his family in class yesterday. Why couldn't Rivers understand that it was not *their* fault the country had an unemployment problem? Everyone always had to go looking for easy answers.

The acrid smell of smoke suddenly reached Jack's nose. As he hurried out of the toilet block he saw his bag, complete with all his folders and expensive text books, on fire. Rivers! It *had* to be.

Rivers and Bolton ambled past, sniggering.

'If things are getting too *hot* for you, slope-head, you can always go home!' jeered Bolton.

Jack kicked at his bag, trying to extinguish the flames, but it was too late. His control snapped.

'You're going to pay for this!' he screamed.

'Wooohhh, like I'm really scared,' said Rivers, examining his fingernails.

'What have I ever done to you, anyway?' asked Jack. His bag and his precious science folders were now just a smouldering mess.

Rivers swaggered up to him and quietly took hold of the front of his jacket.

'You and me've got a lot of unfinished business, slope,' he said, softly.

Jack bristled, and pushed his hand away. This was war. 'Yeah. And I'm ready to finish it. After school.'

Rivers laughed. This would be a pushover. 'See you there then, mate,' he said, thumping two fingers on Jack's slight chest. He turned to his henchmen. 'Come on guys, let's move to where the air doesn't stink like dim sims.'

Jack watched them saunter off, Bolton and Johnno practising their left-hooks. Well, he'd done it now. He just hoped all those years of martial arts training from his father would finally pay off.

At lunchtime, the gang hit Ruby's, the cafe opposite the school. It was a comfortable, relaxed sort of a place, with exposed brick walls and arches, and inviting, intimate booths. Pinball machines and video games flanked the back wall, and a row of pool tables kept customers occupied. Ruby herself, a large, middle-aged, no-nonsense type of woman, presided over the place with a proprietorial eye. There wasn't much that got past Ruby.

Nick was happy. School was a non-event for an hour, he had a cold drink in his hand, his feet up, and a pool game with Con coming up. What more could he ask for?

Then he saw Jodie, sitting alone over at the counter, sipping a juice. He wondered what she'd thought of the stunt he'd pulled that morning. Surely she must be getting the message by now! If only he could think of a way of getting close to her.

He spotted two girls from his class, Chaka and Rose, and waved frantically at them. He'd seen them chatting to Jodie at recess, and needed to pick their brains.

'Where's the fire?' asked Rose, flicking back her long, streaky brown hair. She slid into the booth beside him, popping a piece of gum into her mouth. She wasn't going to take any nonsense from Nick. He probably only wanted to borrow money anyway.

'You were talking to that Jodie chick before, weren't you?'

'Yeah, so?' said Rose. Personally, she'd thought the girl was a bit up herself. She popped her gum.

'Well, what's she into?' asked Nick.

'Why?' asked Chaka, suspiciously, her dark eyes glinting in the dim light of the cafe.

'Why do you think?' asked Nick.

'What's it worth?' countered Chaka.

'Come on,' wheedled Nick. 'I'm always helping you two out with info about guys.'

Rose pulled a face. That'd be the day!

'She must have told you something,' said Nick, pushing Con away. Con was eager to start the pool-game and was in his face.

'Ah – I think she likes music,' volunteered Chaka.

Music, huh? thought Nick. He lightly tugged Chaka's glossy plait. 'Thanks,' he said simply. 'I owe you one.'

Nick left Con jumping up and down on the spot, brandishing his pool cue, and slid across the floor to the empty stool beside Jodie, neatly cutting off Ben Barnes who was about to sleaze onto it. He turned to face Jodie, flashing the Poulos family heritage – white, evenly-spaced teeth.

'Hi, how's it going?' he asked.

Jodie stared straight ahead. 'Okay – until you came along.'

Unfazed, Nick ploughed ahead. 'I heard you were into music.'

Jodie shrugged.

Nick edged a little closer. 'So am I.'

Jodie lifted an eyebrow. 'Oh yeah? What?'

Nick relaxed. He was on the home stretch now. 'Oh, you know, Chili Peppers, Pearl Jam . . . '

Jodie smiled archly at her reflection in the cafe mirror. 'Yeah, right. I thought so.'

Nick's heart skipped a beat. Yes! 'You like them too?' he asked confidently.

Jodie fixed him with a look that could kill cockroaches at sixty paces. 'No.'

She stood up, handing him her empty juice bottle. 'They make me want to throw up.'

Shaken, but not defeated, Nick threw in a final salvo. 'So, how would you feel about going out with me some time?'

Jodie gave him a couple of seconds to feel optimistic about her answer before finally crushing him. 'Same way I feel about your music,' she said, before heading out the door, back to school.

Nick watched her leave. Damn! He'd stuffed it up again.

He'd tried being cool, being romantic, being charming – what was it going to take to get a girl like Jodie interested in him?

It hadn't taken long for word about the fight between Rivers and Jack to filter around the school. By the time Jack had put his books away and walked out to the appointed place – behind the toilet block – half the school had lined up, gunning for blood.

Rivers and his mates were already waiting. Rivers took his cap off and handed it to Bolton, who silently crushed it in his fist.

'This is going to be that cat-eater's face, man,' he said, grinning up at Rivers. 'Mate – you are going to cream this guy.'

Rivers flexed his biceps. 'Shouldn't be a problem.'

Johnno looked up and saw Jack approaching, his shoulders straight. 'You gotta watch these slopes, mate. They don't always fight fair ...'

Rivers silenced him with a look. 'You and Bolton are going to be there for me, though, aren't you ...?'

Johnno exchanged grins with Bolton, then smashed his fist into the palm of his other hand. 'Ma-ate. You want backup, you got it!'

Nick saw Jack heading for the toilets and rushed to try and talk him out of the fight. 'This guy means business,' he said, pushing Con, who'd reached Jack before him and was offering his services as coach, out of the way. 'You can always back out, you know.'

'No,' said Jack, doggedly. 'I have to fight him.'

'Yeah mate,' said Con, dancing around and filling the air with a series of mock punches. 'And you know, we'll all be

24

there to back you up. Steve, Nick, whoever you want!'

'No,' said Jack, quietly. 'It's my fight. I'll fight him alone.'

Nick had to admire his courage. He whistled softly. 'So you're really going through with it, then?'

Jack looked over at Rivers, then back to Nick. 'I have to. If I don't, he'll just keep on pushing.'

Nick wished him luck. He just hoped Rivers was willing to treat this as a fair fight. He'd seen him and his mates in action before, and it wasn't a pretty sight.

Rivers was getting agitated. He'd been staring Jack out for the last few minutes and the wimp was just standing his ground, staring back. Well, he'd had enough. He'd teach him and his people a lesson.

He prodded Jack on the shoulder. 'Well, what are you waiting for?' Jack's lack of response infuriated him. He lunged at him, knocking him off balance, and sent him sprawling onto the asphalt, giving him a swift kick to the ribs for good measure. The crowd erupted. The fight was on!

Through a wall of pain, Jack heard the voices of the crowd urging him on. It would be easy, so easy, to give up now, admit defeat. Rivers was physically much bigger and heavier than him. But then he saw his face, with that look he'd seen so many times on faces on people in the street. People who didn't even know him or his family, who just wanted them out of their country. But he'd done nothing wrong. And neither had his people. They were just the newest arrivals in a long chain of migrants from different countries. It was time to stand up for himself.

He picked himself up from the ground, the blood surging to his temples. The voices of Nick and Danielle behind him gave him the courage to make his first move. But instead of a smashing punch, it was a deft kick with his foot to the side of Rivers' head. Now it was Rivers' turn to go sprawling, straight into the arms of Con and Steve. They eagerly pushed him back into the ring for more punishment.

Jack focused his attention on Rivers' face. The louse didn't look quite so confident now, not after that kick. He winced as a rain of punches landed on his face, drawing blood from his nose and lip. Scumbag. He dreaded to think what his father would say when he came home with his face bruised and bloody. He tensed, poised to deliver another kick. But before he could line it up correctly, he felt a sharp stab of pain to his ankle as an errant foot – one of Rivers' mates, no doubt – tripped him up. He found himself examining the texture of the asphalt for the second time that afternoon, while Rivers danced about, laughing.

It was too much for Con. He'd seen the whole thing. He plunged headlong into the circle, making a beeline for Bolton's ugly red neck. Rivers beat him to it, clobbering Con and sending him flying. It was like a red rag to a bull. Half a dozen of Con's mates, sweating on the sidelines for a piece of the action, jumped into the fray, with Nick punching and pummelling the hardest of the lot.

Chaka and Rose stood cheering them on from the sidelines. Suddenly, Chaka held her breath. A new player had entered the arena – a slim blonde one. Miss wasn't going to try and break it all up, was she – not by herself? Chaka looked around for Southgate and the other heavies on the staff. No-one. Not a sausage.

'Miss!' she called. 'Don't...' But it was too late. She watched, trance-like, as Nick's arm swung up, his fist ready to crunch into Rivers' face. Instead, it connected neatly with the anxious face of his teacher, Ms Milano. She went spinning across the circle, collapsing finally in a crumpled little heap on the ground.

'*Madre de Dios*,' gasped Chaka, crossing herself. Poor Miss. Poulos was really for it now.

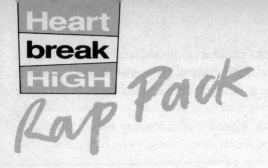

Chapter Four

'As far as I'm concerned, the incident in the school ground yesterday is in the past – finished. I want us all to make a new start. But I will say this. I don't care who you are, or where you come from, or what language you speak, or what colour you are. I will not tolerate you physically or verbally harassing any other person. And that includes me. Do I make myself clear?'

The words of Ms Milano's speech had echoed around the walls of the silent classroom, infiltrating even the most resistant minds in her class. They'd been frightened and ashamed – the lot of them – when she was hurt, and then they'd come to school the next morning and found her quietly setting up her desk, a large, purplish bruise disfiguring her sweet features. And no-one had been more ashamed than Nick. After all, he'd been the one to put it there, hadn't he?

Nick couldn't believe that she hadn't lagged on him for decking her. That had really meant a lot to the rest of the kids as well. It had been a real gesture of solidarity towards them – something these kids didn't often experience. It had earned her their respect. They quit giving her a hard time in class.

In fact the fight had been something of a turning point for several people at Hartley High. Rivers actually stopped hassling Jack for a while. It was almost as though he admired the guy for standing up to him. Or maybe he was ashamed – though he'd never admit it – about Ms Milano getting hurt during a fight he'd instigated. Jack took this as a sign, however limited, of acceptance. It was a relief to know no more incidents like the bag-burning affair were likely to happen. He settled down to work, earning enthusiastic praise from his teachers. Maybe he could become a doctor after all!

The soccer games continued, of course – Rivers would never be able to wipe them out. There were just too many kids at the school whose parents came from soccer-playing countries. And now a new sound could be heard in the playground . . .

Con and Nick and the rest of the gang arrived at school one morning to find a knot of kids gathered around Jodie, who'd set up a boom box near the canteen. A grungy drum rhythm thumped out, while Jodie danced around the speakers, rapping:

Yo! Dad was doin' time when my mother pulled the scam
Started doin' pushups on the cold bitumen
Ever since that day I been cruisin' around
It seems that everywhere I go the sucker starts to burn down.

Rose pulled a face. 'Check the lyrics. Who does she think she is?'

'Shut your face, Rose,' said Nick, his eyes fixed on Jodie. 'This is good stuff.'

29

Mother's in heaven, diggedy dad's lost his load
My older sister props a doorway up in Darlinghurst Road
Apology Biology – in petrol I will douse
So check yourself before I burn down this wacked house.

'Wicked!' said Con, jumping up to join Jodie as she reached the chorus:

The roof is on fire. Burn! Burn!
The school is on fire. Burn! Burn!

Jodie tossed her head and pranced around, enjoying the attention she was getting. So far, most of the losers at this school had been pretty cool towards her. Except for Nick, of course. He'd been all over her like a lovesick puppy. He was kind of cute, though. Great buns. If only he didn't try so hard! She made a mental note to tell him about it some day.

More and more of the kids were joining in with her rap, jumping up and punching the air every time she sang 'Burn!' They looked like they were enjoying it too. Well, who wouldn't? This place was such a dump anything that created a diversion would go down well. She was sick of moving. Sick of dump schools. Anyway, she had a good voice, so why shouldn't she show it off sometimes?

She was just starting out on the third verse when her chem. teacher, Mr Southgate, appeared out of nowhere, raving on about the disturbance she was creating. Disturbance! Huh – he could talk.

'That'll be enough of that rubbish,' shouted Southgate, reaching out to flick the switch on her boom box. He silenced the booing crowd, then turned to face Jodie. 'I'm waiting for an explanation.'

Jodie pouted. 'For what?'

Southgate moved in close. 'I could've sworn I heard an incitement to arson. Something about "burning down the school"? Perhaps you'd like to give a repeat performance in front of the principal?'

Jodie sighed. Teachers! They were all the same. She watched Nick pushing forward through the crowd.

'Hey!' he said belligerently. 'It's just music.'

Southgate sniggered. 'Ah,' he crowed. 'Poulos the art lover.' He pointed to the boom box. 'You can give me that, now.'

'Get lost,' spat Jodie.

'Can't we say *anything* in this yard?' said Nick. 'Whatever happened to freedom of speech?'

'And since when have you cared, Poulos?'

Jodie looked on with amusement as Nick fought her battle for her. Maybe the guy *did* have his uses.

Nick stood his ground. 'This is our playground. We can say, or sing, whatever we like.'

Southgate moved in closer. 'And how are you going to stop me stopping you?' he purred.

'It's a free country,' said Nick, on a roll now. He'd heard his father talking like this after meetings at the Greek club. 'We've got rights.'

Southgate laughed. 'Your hormones are showing, sport. You'd care deeply about stamp collecting if Little Miss Rap here waved her album about.'

Jodie's hackles rose. It was time she stepped back in, gained control. 'Shove it!' she jeered, making a grab for her boom box. 'You're a neurotic Nazi!'

But she'd overstepped the mark this time. Southgate left Nick alone and whipped round to face her. 'You!' he said, his voice full of menace. 'Principal's office. Now!'

Jodie snorted. So he was sending her on somewhere else, was he? Couldn't he handle his own flak? Well, it wasn't like she'd never seen the inside of a principal's office before.

She couldn't resist getting in one last parting shot, though.

She turned to Nick, gesturing at Southgate with her thumb. 'See? This is what happens when cousins marry!'

Nick watched her strut away, head held high. Man, this chick was really something!

Danielle watched from the classroom window as Jodie slammed off to Principal Deloraine's office. Poser. What had the words said? Something about her being 'born in the gutter.' As if. And then all of that wank about burning down the school. She wasn't sure exactly what had gone down with Southgate, but by the look on his face it had been fairly major. Well, she was in for it now. Probably get suspended or something.

Nick burst into the room, shouting about Southgate.

'Just take your seat quietly please, Nick,' said Ms Milano. 'It's bad enough that you're late.'

Nick refused to sit down till he'd said his piece. 'Southgate sucks, Miss,' he whined. 'You saw what happened in the yard, didn't you?'

'Can you save it for later, please?'

Nick sat down, slamming his fist onto the desk. 'It's not fair, miss! We should be able to listen to what we want in the yard.'

His teacher sighed. She thought she'd sorted this sort of

32

behaviour out already. When were the kids in this class going to lose their aggressive attitude? She was just starting to write some notes on the board when another movement in the room caught her eye. Steve Wiley. Passing a note to Danielle Miller.

Danielle glared at Steve. 'Rack off!' she hissed.

'Would you like to share that note with the class, Steve?' asked Ms Milano, sweetly.

'No,' grunted Steve, mortified. 'It's personal.'

Rivers snatched the note from his hands. 'Hoo hoo!' he laughed. 'Are you reddy for dis? "My darling superspunk Danielle. She meant nothing to me. It's your body I want ..."'

Danielle flinched. Jerk! Now everyone would know her business.

Rose leaned across and patted her shoulder comfortingly. 'What happened?' she mouthed.

'We were at Tony's party and this bimbo was all over him,' whispered Danielle.

Rose looked knowing. 'He's a guy. What do you expect?'

Danielle looked over her shoulder at Steve, who was gazing at her hopefully. She turned back to Rose, her face set.

'Yeah, well you can tell him from me, he's dropped.'

Jodie waited impatiently for Deloraine to begin his lecture. She'd heard it all before. He'd probably rave on for a while about how disappointed he was in her, and then put her on daily reports or something. Typical.

Jim Deloraine finished reading the lyric sheet Bill Southgate had confiscated from Jodie, and frowned. 'Well, Jodie, what have you got to say for yourself?'

Jodie rolled her eyes. 'It's just a song.'

Deloraine fixed her with his 'serious' look. 'I think it's a little more than that. I heard all the carry-on out there. You had half the school chanting along with you.'

'It's close to an incitement to riot,' put in Southgate, flexing his knuckles authoritatively.

'Was this sort of thing allowed at your last school?' asked Deloraine.

Jodie sighed. Cretins. Why did they have to make such a big deal out of everything? 'Look, it's just a song.'

'Really?' said Deloraine. 'Well, it's not the sort of song we encourage in our school. Is that clear?'

Jodie's smile stopped at her mouth. 'Yes, Mr Deloraine.'

'Right, then. Well, I'm putting you on probation this time.'

Jodie's smiled reached her eyes. They *were* all the same. Gutless.

'And if you *are* foolish enough to reoffend,' added Deloraine, 'it will mean an automatic suspension. Now, I want you to see our school counsellor, Ms Fatoush. You seem to be carrying a lot of anger.'

'Yes, Mr Deloraine.' Jodie did a mock curtsey as she left the office.

Jodie sprawled in the chair opposite the counsellor. She'd seen just as many 'social workers' in her time as she had principals. She wondered if this Ms Fatoush would be as much a pushover as all the rest. Probably. The best thing this one had going for her was her hair. She had heaps of it. Thick and bouncy, like those pre-Raphaelite chicks in her art history books.

'So,' said the counsellor, looking Jodie up and down. 'A rapper, hey? Who's your favourite rapper, then – Ice T? Ice Cube? Vanilla Ice?'

34

Jodie smirked. 'Just tell me what I've done wrong, okay?'

Ms Fatoush leaned forward. 'Personally, I don't think you've done *anything* wrong. But I think Mr Southgate is a bit worried about what you're rapping about.'

Jodie tossed her braids. 'Yeah? Well, you can stop me talking, but you can't stop me thinking.'

The counsellor sighed. 'Jodie, I'm not trying to stop you doing anything, okay? Look, Mr Southgate just doesn't understand rap. It's a new thing for him.'

'Yeah, well maybe it's him that needs counselling, not me. Nazi.'

Ms Fatoush tried another tack. 'So how are you settling in generally?'

'I'm all right.'

'Seriously?'

'I'm fine,' snapped Jodie. *Nosy bitch.*

'And how are things with your parents?'

It's time to start spinning it, thought Jodie. Give them what they want to hear. It had been the same at every school she'd been to. Just because she'd been a bit of a handful – a bit *wild* – the teachers and school counsellors had run around flapping their beaks like mother birds, delving into her family background, looking for skeletons in the closet. It was as though they'd learnt in some educational psychology course somewhere that off-the-wall behaviour usually meant problems at home; a wicked step-mother or abusive father at least.

Well, the truth was that her family and home life weren't really that much different to that of anyone else that she knew. It wasn't that her parents were saints or anything, they just lived in Dullsville, in the sticks. Her father hauled loads several times a week for an interstate trucking firm, so she'd rarely got to see him. His job had meant that they'd moved around a lot. And her mum was just . . . well, her mum. They'd never got on that well. It must have been a family failing. Jodie and her sister Linda had split town together as soon as Linda had gotten enough cash together to rent a flat in Sydney. She was waitressing now, in a cafe in Darlinghurst Road.

Linda had made Jodie promise to stay at school as long as she could hack it – there wasn't much future in unloading people's leftovers into grotty dishwashers, she reckoned. Well, so far she'd managed to keep her promise. She'd left her last school with a slight nudge from the principal – he hadn't approved of her clothes sense or her attitude. That was one thing that she quite liked about Hartley High – at least some of the kids knew how to dress. A few of them even showed signs of radical behaviour! It was a pity that the dead-arse teachers couldn't follow suit.

She hadn't quite worked out yet what category Ms Fatoush fell into – 'genuinely interested' or 'preachy do-gooder.' It was best to play it safe. She looked up sullenly and told her a good story, painting a picture of a classic text-book case – Mum was dead, her sister a hooker, her father too boozed to get out of bed. That ought to give the nosy ferret something to think about for a while.

She uncrossed her legs and popped her gum. 'Can I go now?'

Yola Fatoush sighed. 'Yeah, go on, out of here. And no more upsetting Mr Southgate, okay?' She watched Jodie swivel off down the corridor. Either this girl was one tough cookie, or a hell of a liar!

The gang hit Ruby's after school. Con grabbed a stool between Nick and Steve. Ordering a can of drink from Ruby, he took a long draught, then belched. 'Ah, that's better,' he said, rubbing his stomach meditatively. 'You know what, Nick? I've been thinking. What we need is a school soccer team.'

Nick grunted non-committally.

'Mate, are you listening?' asked Con. 'This is important.' He turned to Steve. 'What's wrong with him?'

'What?' said Steve, lost in thought.

'What's with you two anyway?' asked Con, spinning on his stool. He watched Steve's face as Rose and Danielle came in and flopped down in the booth in the corner.

'Oh, I get it,' said Con, shaking his head, wisely. 'You got girl problems. I might be able to help you out, you know?'

'Yeah,' muttered Steve, into his coffee. Nothing that he could see was going to get him out of this one.

Nick jumped off his stool and squeezed into the booth beside Rose. 'Hey, you know what we oughta do, Rose?'

'I give up. What?'

'We oughta publish Jodie's rap in the school newspaper.'

Rose raised her eyebrows. '"We"?'

'Okay, you. You're the editor.' He swept his hand across the table. 'I can see the headline now: PRINCIPAL CAN'T BEAT RAP.'

'Oh yeah,' said Rose, flipping a coaster at him. 'Well I can see another. JODIE PAIN IN BUM, SAYS EDITOR.'

'Come on,' said Nick. 'It's not just her. It's the principle involved, you know?'

'Yeah, sure. As if. And what's in it for you?'

'Nothing. It's the principle, all right? The principle of free speech in a democracy.'

Rose choked on her cappuccino.

'Hey, man. I'm Greek,' said Nick, offended. 'It's in the blood.'

'Yeah, Nick, and I'm Lebanese. We burn it at night to keep away mozzies.'

Danielle, tired of hanging around, stood up to leave. 'Look, Southgate did us a favour, shutting her down like that. She's just a pose.'

Nick rapped the table in front of Rose. 'Oh yeah? So what's next? What happens if they don't like something *you* put in the paper?'

He had her now. Rose stared at him. 'They wouldn't dare.'

'Think about it. If they won't let us *say* what we like, why would they let us read it?'

'But the paper's different,' countered Rose.

Nick sat back, arms folded, his point made. 'Only one way to find out, isn't there?'

Over at the counter, Con was doing his best to cheer up Steve. If he could get him happy again, get his mind off this grief with Danielle, maybe they could put some time in on what was *really* important. Soccer!

'Don't worry, mate,' he wheedled, a Dodgy Brothers clone. 'She likes you. She hates your guts but she *likes* you.'

Steve stirred his third coffee moodily. 'Great. Like that's what I want to hear.'

Con pushed up his shirt-sleeves, ready for action. He flashed a winning smile at Steve. 'What you need, mate, is a go-between.'

'A what?'

'A go-between, mate. It's a big tradition in my country. In Greece, everything – the courtship, the proposal, the reception band, the *honeymoon* arrangements, everything! – is arranged for the lucky man and chick by a marriage-broker.' He inspected his fingernails. 'I can be this for you, you know? A professional.'

Steve winced. 'How much?'

Con backed off, deeply offended. 'Who said anything about money?'

Steve looked hopeful. Maybe . . . 'Will you do it for nothing?'

Con twiddled with his mobile. 'I would if I could, mate . . .', he stroked a few buttons, '. . . but I've got overheads. You know?'

Steve looked over at the empty space where Danielle had been sitting and sighed, defeated. 'Okay. How much?'

Con leaned in closer. 'I got special rates for special mates,' he whispered.

'And what if this doesn't work?'

Con leaned back, satisfied. He was on the way to closing yet another deal. 'I'll only charge you for expenses.'

Steve flipped some coins down onto the counter for his coffees and stood up. 'They didn't call you Con for nothing, did they?'

'Geez, Nick, you better be sure about this,' said Rose, accessing the newspaper file on the computer. They were in the back office behind the English room, where the school paper was produced.

'Hey, what is this?' asked Nick. 'A newspaper editor putting a price on free speech?'

'Yeah, well I just better get an invite to the wedding.'

'Get out of here,' said Nick. He inserted a pile of paper in the printer. 'Jodie's got nothing to do with this. I told you, it's the *principle*.'

'Yeah, well this stuff in the rap all better be true,' said Rose, typing furiously. She pressed print, waited for the copies to emerge, then, pulling the first page off the top of the pile, showed Nick the headline. 'What do you reckon?'

Nick studied the page. 'RAP CLAMPDOWN: A SIGN OF THINGS TO COME???'

'Hey, that's great, Rose!'

'Of course, it's great,' snapped Rose. 'That's why I'm the editor.' She grabbed a pile of copies from the printer, and handed them to Nick. 'Okay, here's your half. Now get them out there.'

The special issue of the paper spread around the school like free tickets to a Nirvana concert. The students had got off on Jodie's rap and wanted more. Nick proudly presented Jodie with a personal copy in the corridor.

'Hey, wow!' said Jodie, reading the copy. 'Cool.'

Nick smiled modestly. 'It was my idea.'

Danielle snatched a copy from Nick, her nose wrinkling with disgust as she read the words. 'Burn down the school. That's like real revolutionary stuff, mate.'

'Everyone's a critic,' said Jodie, locking horns.

Danielle smirked and tapped the page. 'Have you thought about what the teachers are going to say about this, Nick?'

'They're going to love it!' said Nick, surprised. 'It's poetry, that's all.'

'You reckon?' said Danielle. 'Then why is Southgate taking a copy into Deloraine's office as we speak?'

Nick peered down the corridor. Oh oh. Danielle was right. But hey. Who cared? It was just a rap. The teachers were always going on about how important it was to think about things and express yourself. So that was just what they were doing. Expressing themselves. Wasn't it?

The next morning, there was evidence of someone's 'free expression' all over the school. Nick and Con arrived to find a group of teachers staring at the charred paint on the brick wall near the breeze-way. Someone had dragged over a metal rubbish bin, stuffed it full of paper and rags, and set fire to it. The wall behind it was covered with graffiti about the school, urging students to 'burn it down'.

Oops. This was not really what Nick had had in mind when he handed out the newspapers. How was he to know some jerk would take the words literally? Once Deloraine found out, he, Rose, Jodie – they'd all be dead meat. He watched Deloraine's car pull into the parking lot with a sinking heart. His father was going to kill him . . .

Chapter Five

Jodie was starting to get used to the decor in Principal Deloraine's office. She checked out the print on the wall while he got stuck into Rose.

'So, as editor, Rose, you stand by what you published?'

Rose looked defiant. 'Yes. I've got the right to publish.' She threw a sidelong glance at Jodie. 'Even if I reckon the rap is a wank,' she added softly.

Deloraine sighed and turned his attention to Jodie. The Poulos boy could wait. 'And you. What have you got to say?'

Jodie shrugged. This was all so boring. 'What about?'

Deloraine's patience took a dive. 'Your attitude is not helping your case,' he snapped. 'Ms Milano – your teacher – thinks I should go easy on you. She – heaven help her – says that we're not meant to take your words "literally".'

So Ms Milano was sticking up for them, was she? thought Jodie. *Well, good for her.* 'People can take them how they like,' she said to Deloraine.

Mr Deloraine ran his fingers through his thick, white hair. *He looks like he'd rather be somewhere else,* thought Jodie. *Well, I'm not going to give him that pleasure just yet.*

42

'Unfortunately,' sighed her principal, 'someone has taken you very literally, and I'm the one who has to deal with the results. I suppose that's not your problem, eh?'

Jodie shrugged. 'I didn't light the fire.'

'No,' admitted Deloraine. 'But you provided the fuel.' He turned his attention to Rose as he delivered his bomb-shell. 'And you know something? It's not going to happen again. Because I'm closing down the school newspaper.'

Rose and Nick looked at each other, stunned.

Deloraine sat down at his desk and began shuffling papers. 'Understand?' The three students facing him nodded mutely. 'Now get out of here!' he yelled.

Tempers in Ms Milano's English class were running hot. Who wanted to discuss dopy Shakespearean wankers when there were important issues at stake? Deloraine's decision to shut down the newspaper had not gone down too well with most of the class.

'It's outrageous,' cried Rose, jumping out of her seat. 'What about freedom of the press?'

'Please sit down, Rose,' said her teacher.

'They can't get away with it,' said Rose, slamming her fist onto the desk.

Ms Milano did her best to defuse the situation. 'Well, we won't get anywhere thumping the table and shouting, will we?' she asked. She extended an invitation to the rest of the class. 'Come on, I'd like to hear some reasoned argument.'

Con jumped up. 'Well, I'm as mad as hell and I'm not gonna take it any more.' The class laughed. Ms Milano waved him down. 'Anyone else?' she asked. 'Nick?'

Nick thought for a moment, then spoke. 'Hey. This isn't just about a rap song. This is our paper. All of us.' He looked around the room, searching for support. 'We've got a right to have a voice. So what are we going to do about it?'

Rivers raised his fist. 'Nothing!' he yelled. Nick gave him the finger.

Rose waited for the noise following Rivers' outburst to die down, then tried a new tack. 'What about a petition?'

Danielle groaned. 'That'll really scare the pants off them.'

Rose was adamant. 'If we get enough names it will.'

Con butted in. 'Can we sign it more than once?'

The class broke up again. Nick stood up, his face flushed. 'So we're going to do nothing, uh?' He scanned the faces in the room.

Rivers and Bolton looked at each other, then sat back with their arms folded. 'Yeah,' they said, sniggering.

Nick sat down again, defeated. At least they could have *tried* to do something ...

Suddenly, a quiet voice entered the discussion. Chaka. Her face was a study in determination. 'We have to fight,' she said simply.

The class turned to look at her. Chaka *never* spoke up in class.

Chaka stood her ground. 'If you don't fight,' she said, her voice gaining strength, 'you get nothing.'

Rivers groaned. 'Go home, will ya?' he said.

Jack jumped in to Chaka's defence. He knew exactly where she was coming from. They'd worked together on a group project for Social Studies about their family backgrounds. He'd found out that her family came from El Salvador, and had suffered their own personal tragedy. He'd told her about his brother, Duc, and she'd confided to him that her father

44

Nick
played by Alex Dimitriades

Jodie
played by Abi Tucker

Con
played by Salvatore Coco

Rivers
played by Scott Majors

Steve
played by Corey Page

Jack
played by Tai Nguyen

Danielle
played by Emma Roche

Rose
played by Kathy Halliday

Chaka
played by Isabella Gutierrez

was missing as well, somewhere in the depths of El Salvador, fighting for the rights of his people. It was something that no-one else at school knew, not even her best friend, Rose. The secret knowledge was like a bond between them.

'Shut up and listen,' he said to Rivers, the memory of Chaka's confidence burning him. 'She knows what she's talking about.'

Rivers muttered something nasty in return, too softly for anyone to hear the actual words. But his intent was clear.

Chaka smiled over at Jack, then turned back to Rivers. Each word was like a bullet. 'You,' she said, 'you give up so easy. Well, one day, you're gonna lose it all.' She paused for a moment, thinking of her father. Sometimes it was hard to remember what his face looked like. 'And then ...' she went on, finally, '... then you'll wish you'd fought.'

She sat down amidst cheers and whistles. Ms Milano looked at her English class with new eyes. They'd never been big on discussion before. Well, at last they'd found something to get fired up about.

At lunchtime, Rose did the rounds of the schoolground with the hastily drawn-up petitions, asking kids for signatures. When she passed one to Danielle to sign, her friend screwed up her nose. As far as she was concerned, Jodie's rap had been nothing more than a bid for attention. Besides, she had problems of her own to deal with. She saw Con mooching around with a soccer ball, and wandered over.

'So how much is Steve paying you?' she asked, not realising how close she'd come to the truth.

Con's face was a mask of innocence. 'Who said anything about Steve?'

'Not me,' said Danielle. 'I don't want to know about the

two-timing jerk. In fact, you can tell him from me he's a dag. He dresses like a slob. He's got no style ... and he couldn't write a decent love letter to save his life. When's he going to grow up?'

Con nodded sagely. 'Ah, Danni, the course of true love never runs smooth.'

Danielle stared at him for a moment, then flounced off. These guys were as bad as each other! Serious head cases. 'Plus he's got dopey mates!' she threw back over her shoulder.

Nick's parents were less than impressed to find he was once again in trouble at school.

'Sounds pretty serious, Nick,' said his father, helping himself to another serve of moussaka. 'They don't ban newspapers for nothing, you know. So what's happening this time?'

Nick looked uncomfortable. His father could be pretty hard to talk to at times. 'Look, there's this girl ...' he began.

His father put down the serving spoon. 'Ah. I knew there'd be a girl involved somewhere.'

His little sister smirked. 'So did I!'

Nick struggled to explain. 'She wrote this song, see, about burning the school down. We printed it in the paper and some idiot lit a fire.'

His father's face turned red. 'Well, what do you expect? I mean, kids are influenced by that sort of thing! Why on earth does this girl want to write a song about burning the school down in the first place?'

Nick was startled by his father's reaction. He wished he'd never opened his mouth. 'It was just in a garbage bin,' he hedged. 'It wasn't dangerous.'

'Big fires start from little ones,' said his father.

Nick bristled. Why did his father always have to be so negative about everything? 'That's not the point!' he yelled. 'If they get away with banning our paper, what's next? Soon we won't be able to say anything! We've got to take a stand.'

His father banged his fist on the table, startling Effie. 'I don't want you fooling around with this stuff. You hear me! You're always fooling around. If it's not soccer then it's girls or something else. Anything but your education!' His tone changed. 'Tell me, why is this suddenly so important now?'

Nick stared moodily down at his plate. 'Just forget about it, all right?'

But his father was not to be put off. Ignoring the requests of his wife that they get on with their meal, he continued to yell and shout at his son. Children! All they ever did was bring home problems for him to deal with.

Con caught up with Steve and passed on the bad news.

'You're in serious trouble with this chick, mate,' he told him sadly. He ticked off the points on his fingers. 'She thinks you're a grub, you're a slob, you're a pig ...'

Steve looked mournful. 'So what you're saying is, I'm history, right?'

'Well, look at it this way, mate. You've got an image problem.'

Steve looked perplexed. 'I can't believe she said I was a slob ...' he muttered. He trailed off as he saw Danielle heading over with Nick, Jodie and Rose. Rose's face was mutinous.

'What's the problem?' he asked her.

'It's the petitions,' she said. 'Someone's screwed us up. Signed more than once, or used false names. Deloraine won't accept them.' She looked at him closely. 'You didn't, did you?' she asked, threateningly.

Steve gulped. 'No way!'

'Well the paper's definitely gone now,' said Rose. 'Kaput.'

Jodie looked at Rose. 'So how come you didn't check the signatures?' she asked.

'How come you didn't?' Rose fired back.

Jodie glowered. 'It's not my department.'

'So what is your department?' asked Danielle, sweetly.

Jodie was sick of Danielle's constant bitching. 'Chill out, will you? It wasn't my idea to put the rap in the paper!'

'You seemed pretty pleased at the time,' observed Rose, causing Jodie to totally lose it.

'I didn't mean it to happen,' she yelled, 'so get off my case!'

Steve watched the ruffling of feathers despondently. Chicks. He'd never understand them. He caught Danielle's eye. 'Did you really say I was a slob?' he asked sadly. But Danielle only tossed her head, leaving him in agony.

Nick, who'd been silent up till now, suddenly fired up. Yes! What a brilliant idea! Chuckling, he had a quiet word with Con and Rose. Maybe the newspaper wasn't quite down for the count yet ...

With Con and Nick standing guard outside, Rose snuck into the newspaper office, and began tapping out a special, *special* issue of the *Hartley Flash*. She'd been voted in as editor by the students and she was damn well going to let them know what was going down around the school. She laughed, picturing Deloraine's face when he saw she'd defied him. So he thought he could close down the newspaper and take away their right to free speech, did he? Well, he had another think coming ...

Being banned certainly did a lot for a paper's circulation, thought Nick, as he watched the large pile of papers dwindle in a matter of minutes. It seemed *everybody* wanted a copy of the underground edition of the *Flash*.

'Read all about it!' he called to the passing students. 'Banned newspaper lives!'

Rose joined in. 'Hot off the press! Latest underground issue lifts lid on freedom of speech scandal.'

A mob of Year 8 students raced over for their copies. Jodie, seeing the attention they were getting, grabbed a pile of papers and began touting them as well. 'Extra! Extra!' she called. 'Student property stolen in boom box ban.'

Nick blanched as a middle-aged woman snatched his last copy.

'Who was that?' asked Jodie.

'Principal's secretary,' said Nick, feeling less confident than he looked. 'I guess it's really going to hit the fan now.'

Twenty minutes later, Deloraine was in full bore. They were silly, irresponsible children, he told them. And they were in definite trouble this time. Big trouble. He came down particularly hard on Jodie, who was finally starting to wilt under pressure.

'You must realise, Jodie,' he said, 'that you're the one the other students are going to blame for this unfortunate chain of events. Look at the trouble you've gotten your friends into! You have to take responsibility for what you create.'

Nick jumped in. 'We're making our own decisions on this, sir.'

Deloraine fixed his gaze on Nick. 'Really? And how likely is this threat of a sit-in strike?'

49

He watched Nick falter slightly. 'We ... we think our claims are legitimate, sir.'

Deloraine sighed. 'Look, I know how you feel,' he said. 'I worked on a student newspaper once. I know how difficult it can be when there are things you want to say, or feelings you want to express.'

Nick squared his shoulders. It was time he showed Deloraine they meant what they'd set out to do. 'Look, sir, we're serious about this. And we know the students are behind us. Basically, you have until twelve o'clock tomorrow to lift the ban, or we go on strike.' He looked over at Rose for confirmation of this. She nodded.

'I see,' said Deloraine, stroking his chin. 'And I can't persuade you to change your minds?'

Nick, Rose and Jodie all shook their heads.

'All right then,' said Deloraine. 'Well, let me give you a deadline. As of noon tomorrow, if you have not withdrawn your threat to strike, retracted your claims, and apologised, you are all suspended from school for a week.'

Rose bit her lip. So it had come to this.

Deloraine picked up the boom box from the shelf behind him and handed it to Jodie. 'Now get out of here, the lot of you. And take that thing with you!'

Jodie mooched out into the street, glad to finally see the end of the day at school. 'Heartbreak High' was right, all right. Whoever had given it that name had known what they were talking about.

Nick caught up with her. 'You okay?' he asked, concerned.

'I wish I'd never written the poxy rap now,' said Jodie.

'Hey, it's not your fault, all right?' said Nick. 'I mean, this whole situation was just waiting to happen, sooner or later. They can't just push us around like that.' He took her hand.

Jodie stopped walking and turned to look up at him. Her eyes were teary. 'It's funny, you know. All that stuff about my parents? Well, none of it's true. Dad's just a truckie, my sister's a waitress ... and my mother's not dead, either.'

Nick gently touched her cheek. 'So why did you write it?' he asked.

'I don't know,' said Jodie. 'I'm scared, I guess. About making friends. Getting to know people. I've only been here two weeks, and I've already put everybody off.'

Nick's face moved closer to Jodie's. 'You haven't put me off,' he whispered. He reached out and pulled her towards him, lightly brushing his lips against her mouth. Jodie pulled back for a moment, then returned the kiss. Life could be so complicated, sometimes. It felt good to be held, if only for a moment.

She broke off the kiss and smiled crookedly up at Nick.

'What's wrong?' he whispered, stroking her hair.

'I just want some friends,' said Jodie, simply.

Nick gave her a hug. 'Sure,' he said, 'easy. How many do you want?'

Jodie grinned. Nick was fun. Maybe life at Heartbreak High wasn't going to be so bad after all. Twining her arms around Nick's neck, she moved back in for a repeat performance.

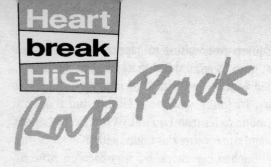

Chapter Six

Nick and Jodie caught up with the rest of the gang at Ruby's. Nick wasn't expecting the wall of opposition that greeted him. Most of the kids were put off taking part in the strike by the thought of a week of suspension. He couldn't understand it. Okay, so it would look bad on their school records, but there was a bigger issue at stake here, wasn't there? Surely they could see that?

Danielle was the most vocal in her opposition. She pointed her chin towards Jodie. 'Why should we carry the can for *her*?' she snapped.

Steve agreed with her. It just wasn't worth getting suspended for. What was in it for *them*?

Con was ... being Con. 'I'm in,' he said confidently. 'If you mention the soccer team for sure.'

Nick groaned. What had happened to solidarity? They were all suddenly being about as useful as Jason Donovan at a death metal gig.

'Look,' he said. 'I thought we all agreed that having our say was important. So what's changed now?'

Jack and Chaka exchanged guilty glances.

'You going to jump every time Southgate tells you to?' went on Nick. 'For once we were all together ... all of us. And they had to listen to what we were saying. And that felt good. Very good.'

He looked around the circle of friends. Noticing that some of them were starting to waver, he continued. 'We've got to stand up for our say now ...' he paused for effect, 'or shut up forever.'

That had got them thinking. He could see it in their faces. Jack was with him, and Chaka; even Rose – who had really strict parents – and Steve looked like they were coming round. That just left Danielle.

She looked around at her friends as, one by one, they agreed to participate in the strike. 'Oh well,' she said finally, smiling up at Nick. 'Not much fun being on your own. Guess I'm in too.'

Yes! Nick was rapt. As long as he had a solid core of people involved, he knew a lot of other kids around the school would join in. He couldn't wait to show Southgate and Deloraine exactly what he thought of their ban.

There was one hurdle still to cross, however. His parents. If he was going to get suspended, it was probably best he gave them a bit of warning beforehand.

As soon as he got home from school, Nick went straight to his bedroom and unpacked his text books, putting in a couple of hours on his homework. That should impress his father, he calculated. Then, at dinner-time, he made sure that he was extra helpful in the kitchen, offering to set the table and helping his mother serve the meal. He waited till his father's stomach was full before he dropped his bombshell.

'I'm probably getting suspended tomorrow, okay? For a week.'

His mother dropped the fork she was holding.

'Why?' barked his father.

'We're going on strike,' said Nick.

'Oh yes,' jibed Mr Poulos. 'And I suppose this girl is involved.'

Nick decided to take the direct approach. 'Yes, she is.' He appealed to his mother. 'I like her. She's opened my eyes to a few things.'

His mother looked at him doubtfully for a moment, then smiled. 'She must be very special.'

But his father wasn't to be fobbed off so easily. 'Okay, so what is this strike about?'

Nick looked him in the eye. 'It's about our voice at school. They want to take it away. Shut us up.'

His father shook his head. 'I don't want you to throw your future away, over a . . . a . . .'

Nick fired up. When was his father going to change the record? 'I'm not throwing anything away!' he yelled, getting up from the table.

His father stopped him with a look. His voice was like ice. 'What if I forbid you? You will defy me, like your headmaster?'

Nick wavered. He didn't want to upset his father he had a deep respect for him – but there were certain things he needed to make clear to him. Otherwise it would continue to be the same old story, with his father calling the shots at every turn. Couldn't he understand that his son had to be allowed to make his own decisions sometimes?

'I can't back down now, Dad,' he said evenly. 'Look, okay, I know I'm not perfect. I've lied to you, gone behind your back sometimes, but I've always listened to what you said. Always.'

54

His father looked at him carefully. 'Go on,' he said.

Nick chose his next words carefully. 'Look, this is hard for me to say. But on this . . . this strike . . .' He held his father's gaze. It was now or never. 'If you force me, yes, I will defy you.'

'They're strong words, Nick,' his father said, shaking his head.

'Well at least I'm saying them to your face.'

Nick's father turned to his wife. He searched her face for a look of approval, and when it came, asked his son to come back to the dinner table.

'All right,' he said finally. 'If you truly believe in this strike, then go ahead. Do it.' He nodded at his wife, who smiled back at him. 'We support you.'

Nick flushed, happy at last. He'd actually broken through to the the old man! If only Deloraine and Southgate could be made to see reason so easily . . .

At the end of period four, Nick and Jodie stashed their books in their lockers, and waited for the rest of the gang to join them. Together, they headed for the corridor outside Deloraine's office, on a nervous high. Sure, they'd all been involved in minor scrapes at one time or another, but none of them had ever defied the principal's authority quite to this extent. A sit-down strike! Maybe they'd get on national television!

Nick made himself comfortable on the linoleum floor under the sporting shields, with Jodie squeezed up next to him. He took her hand. Con settled down opposite them, flanked by Steve and Rose. Con rifled through his bag, searching for something.

'How long's this gonna take?' he asked, expansively. 'I'm a busy man.'

Nick groaned. Con would never change. His face lightened, though, when he saw Jack and Danielle and the rest of the lunchtime soccer crew, plus a heap of kids from Year 10, sit down further along the corridor. Looked like the strike was going to be a success! Any moment now, Deloraine would peep out of his office and see his precious corridor jam-packed with revolting students. The thought was sweet.

It was only a matter of moments before he *did* appear, a frown creasing his forehead. Southgate fell into step beside him. They moved down the corridor till they reached the ringleaders.

'I shall only ask you once,' said Deloraine, his voice tight. 'Please clear this corridor right now.'

Nick looked across at Rose. She held his gaze and shook her head slightly. No-one was going anywhere.

Deloraine stiffened. 'Very well. Nick, Rose, Jodie. As of now you are suspended for a week. Please leave the school grounds.'

The three organisers nervously looked at each other for inspiration. Jodie, her heart thumping wildly, squeezed Nick's hand, and was dismayed to find it was sweating. Finally, Nick took a deep breath. He'd been responsible for getting his friends into this mess. They were relying on him to get them out of it.

'We're on strike because we think we've got the right to express ourselves,' he said, shakily.

His statement was backed up by a round of cheers and whistles. He held out a piece of paper and continued, more confident this time. 'Here is a list of our demands. We're not leaving until they're met.'

Deloraine ignored the piece of paper Nick was waving at him. 'Let me make one thing clear. I will *not* respond to demands. Now you three leave now, or I will have you removed.'

Con grabbed his mobile phone and held it up. 'We'll call Willesee!'

Southgate reached for the mobile. 'I'll take that,' he said smoothly.

Con was disgusted. 'No way!' he yelled, snatching his arm back. The Year 10 students jeered. They had a few bones of their own to pick with Southgate.

Jack leaned over to Rose. 'Check out Deloraine,' he said. 'Look at the colour of his face. I reckon he's going to lose it any second now.'

'Yeah,' said Rose. 'Bet he wished he never got out of bed this morning, eh.'

The colour of Deloraine's face changed from mauve to puce. 'Right!' he snapped. 'You have five minutes to vacate this corridor ... or I will suspend the lot of you.'

The students squealed with mock fear. This was more fun than they'd had in months. Some of them began banging their hands on the floor, like prisoners in a canteen going stir crazy.

Deloraine delivered his parting shot. 'You have been warned!' he spluttered, before retreating to his office. Southgate, his lip curling, followed him, leaving the corridor to the students.

Nick and Jodie hugged each other, eyes shining. Round one to them!

The afternoon wore on. Some of the students were getting bored. Deloraine had ignored them for the past three hours. There were only so many games of 'rock, paper, scissors' you could play.

When Danielle wandered off to the toilets, Con took

advantage of her absence to close his business deal with Steve.

'Look, mate,' he said, making some final scribbles on a grubby piece of paper. 'I've made a list of what it's going to cost you. It's very reasonable.'

Steve studied the list doubtfully.

Con kept up the hard sell. 'So, you want me to place the order? You won't regret it, mate, I promise you. And you know mate, it's Valentine's Day tomorrow. *Very* romantic.' He tapped his nose.

Steve sighed and nodded. How else was he going to get Danielle back? Con picked up his mobile and punched out a number.

'Costa? Con, mate ... *te kanis*. He wants the works, mate.'

Rose watched Con cut his deal and shook her head. He'd never change! She slid herself over to Jodie. It was time to mend some fences.

'Hi,' said Rose.

'Hi,' said Jodie, guardedly.

'Look,' said Rose, 'I know I got pretty heavy yesterday, but I just wanted to say that I'm glad we're all here together now.'

Jodie did a double take. Ms Supercool Editor was actually *apologising* to her? 'Yeah?' she said.

Rose moved a little closer. 'You've got guts. Now all of a sudden we've *all* got guts we never knew we had. It's all down to you.'

Jodie looked pleased. Maybe finally making some friends wasn't going to be that impossible after all! 'Thanks,' she said, genuinely touched by Rose's approach.

Rose smiled back. Maybe this one wasn't such a tough cookie after all! Besides, Nick was usually pretty spot-on about the people he hung out with. The girl must have *something* going for her. She vowed to make an effort to make Jodie feel more like one of the gang from now on.

Con glowered. All this girly touchy-feely stuff was making him sick. Besides, his tummy was rumbling. He checked his watch. 'So what are we doing at 3.30?' he asked Nick.

Nick was unyielding. 'We're not moving, all right!'

Con dropped his bottom lip. 'Can I dial a pizza?'

'Stop thinking about your stomach!' shot back Nick. After such a promising start, the last thing he needed now was their numbers dropping because people's stomachs needed filling.

He looked up to see Ms Milano hurrying along the corridor towards Deloraine's office, a bunch of rolled-up papers in her hand. Something was up ... he wasn't sure what, exactly, but something was about to happen.

At 3.55, Ms Fatoush and Ms Milano asked Rose, Nick and Jodie to accompany them to a nearby classroom, which was still set up with the tables in a circular layout after a discussion session. They'd refused to leave their position on the floor at first, but something about the winks the teachers had given them had got them moving in the end. Nick just hoped that he hadn't compromised their obviously strong position by leaving their post.

Once inside, Ms Milano spread out a sheaf of photocopies on the table. 'You'd better look at these quickly,' she said, checking her watch. 'Mr Deloraine and Mr Southgate will be along in five minutes.'

Nick looked over at Rose, who raised her eyebrows. She didn't have a clue about what was going on either. Nick picked up the first photocopy – a newspaper article. Dated 2 September, 1967, it showed a thin young man dressed in a tie-dyed

T-shirt and flares, his long hair held down with a headband. One hand was clenched in a symbol of rebellion, while the other held a placard screaming STRIKE!

'So?' said Nick, puzzled. 'Who's this supposed to be?'

'Can't you tell?' said Ms Fatoush. 'It's Mr Deloraine. Back in his uni days.'

'Are you kidding?' said Rose, grabbing the photocopy. 'Gimme a look at that.'

'So what was he doing?' asked Nick, impressed.

'According to this,' said Ms Milano, picking up another photocopy, 'he led a group of students who occupied the vice-chancellor's office. Seems like they sat in there for days, refusing to budge. Student politics was pretty hot stuff in the 60s,' she added. 'They didn't automatically have Student Representative Councils like you do nowadays.'

'Wow!' said Nick. He picked up the rest of the pile of papers. 'So what're all these?'

'Articles Mr Deloraine wrote for the uni paper,' Ms Fatoush told him. 'Your headmaster was quite the rebel when he was a student, it seems.'

'So what's the point of all this?' asked Rose, practically.

'We thought it might help speed up the negotiation process a bit,' said Ms Milano. 'We showed these to him just a few minutes ago. Took him for a little trip down memory lane. Reminded him that he hadn't *always* been a principal.' Hearing footsteps in the corridor, she quickly rolled up the papers and stuffed them into her bag. 'I think it might have worked,' she whispered.

Jim Deloraine, backed up by Southgate, walked quietly into the room and sat down. Nick placed a piece of paper on the desk in front of him. 'Here is our list of demands,' he said.

Deloraine sighed. 'I've already made it clear I will not respond to "demands".'

Yola Fatoush stepped in. 'You know, schools are a bit like prisons,' she began thoughtfully. 'They only function via an unwritten agreement between the inmates and the authorities.'

Deloraine coughed. 'I'm not sure I like the notion of students as inmates,' he said.

Ms Fatoush turned to face him. 'Will you concede that if the student body really wants to flip out, there is nothing the staff can do to stop them?'

Deloraine sighed and nodded. 'The option of shooting them is not open to me,' he said, somewhat regretfully.

Christina Milano decided it was time to add her two cents worth. 'Come on, guys, how about a bit of negotiation? Is it possible for any of you to actually *give* a little here?'

Deloraine sighed again and picked up Nick's list of demands. 'I take it this is an ambit claim,' he said finally, placing the list back on the desk. 'You understand we have a few "demands" of our own. An apology to Mr Southgate for starters. And a written retraction.'

Rose laughed mockingly. 'How can we do a written retraction if we haven't got a newspaper?' she asked.

'And what about our suspensions?' added Nick.

'And I want the right to rap,' insisted Jodie.

Deloraine paused. 'And point ten? I don't see what a soccer team has to do with anything.'

'It was democratically included,' argued Nick. Rose held her breath. Looked like they were close to a breakthrough.

Southgate snorted. 'By your cousin?'

Rose and Jodie giggled, breaking the tension in the room. Nick relaxed. Everything was going to be fine. 'Okay,' he conceded. 'It's not a high priority demand.' He moved closer to Deloraine. 'Only you have to agree not to tell Con his suggestion didn't get up. He'll kill me!'

By the time Steve arrived at the school hall for the big Valentine's Day party the next night, celebrations were in full swing. The hall had been decorated with red streamers and pink balloons, while cardboard hearts and cupids – courtesy of the Year Nine art class – covered the walls. Rose was on cloud nine – she had her precious newspaper back – and Nick was feeling pretty proud of himself. It wasn't every student that could stand up to the teachers and win!

Steve adjusted his kiss curls, straightened his medallion and checked the buttons on his sequinned vest. This outfit that Con had organised for him to impress Danielle with had better work. He'd felt like a dork putting it on, but Con had insisted he looked the part.

He cased the crowded hall. The Gangstas, a school band that had been organised by Mr Brown, the music teacher, were setting up, getting ready to play. He watched Nick push a protesting Jodie towards the microphone. Looked like they were in for another rap session.

Finally he saw her. Danielle. It was now or never. Holding out a ginormous bunch of red roses, he approached her, grinning shyly.

Danielle took one look at the overdressed disco king lurching towards her and laughed in spite of herself. He looked like something out of a Greek reception band. At least the moron had made an effort. Her heart melted.

Steve was rapt. 'Ay!' he cried, in a mock Greek accent. ''appy Valentine's Day! Waddyareckon?' Danielle kissed and hugged him, still chuckling, while Con looked on proprietorially. He'd come through with the goods, yet again.

Rose checked out the cuddly couple and laughed. 'Hey, did you see this?' she asked, showing Chaka and Jack a copy of *The Flash*. ' "RAP COOL!" SAYS PRINCIPAL' blazed the headline.

They turned to watch Jodie and Nick step up onto the stage. Jodie grabbed the mike and, with a big grin on her face, began belting out her latest rap. This time, however, everyone joined in on the chorus, including the teachers!

Here I go, here I go, here I go, here I go,
Kickin around for y'all, flippin and divin
Yo it the time and, strivin to party

Get down for V V V Valentine's Day
Raise your hands in the air
Rippin it up to funky stuff
And everybody say go head
Go head go head go head go head go head

Dance, say hey, go Valentine's Day
Dance, say hey, go Valentine's Day
Dance, say hey, go Valentine's Day
Dance, say hey, go Valentine's Day.

Ricketty boom rolling with Cupid
Here I have some
Enough to go round for all you singles in the room some
The bows and arrows back jacking for hearts on Valentine's day
I like it, I love it, yo here we go again.

L to the O to the V to the E
Say Valentine's Day on the M.I.C.
L to the O to the V to the E
Say Valentine's Day on the M.I.C.

Chapter Seven

Nick could have found the music room with his eyes shut. Even though the walls were padded with egg cartons from the Home Eco room, and the door was jammed firmly shut, the squeals of feedback emanating from the room were sharper than the set of six steak knives in the Demtel ad.

He peered in through the tiny pane of glass. Brian, the keyboard player from The Gangstas, was on his knees. Surrounded by snaking lines of leads and cables, he was fiddling with the knobs on the school amplifier. Nick's eyes followed one of the power cords to where it was plugged into a double adaptor, which was plugged, piggyback style, into yet another double adaptor. He was surprised the whole lot hadn't blown up by now.

Jodie was standing impatiently at the microphone, one eye on the clock. She gestured to Nick to come in when she saw him at the window.

'That sounded great,' said Nick, tentatively.

'It sounded like crap!' complained Jodie. 'I can't believe this mouldy piece of equipment they have the hide to call an amp. It looks like it came out of the ark.'

Nick checked out the ancient valve amplifier the school used for practice sessions. It did look a bit like it had just gone three rounds with Schwarzenegger. He winced as it gave out a piercing crackle.

Jodie was looking desperate. 'Can't you do something with it?' she begged Brian. 'This is the only rehearsal time we've got to put this demo together.'

Up until the last ten minutes, Jodie had been feeling great. It looked like her big chance to crack it in the music world had finally arrived.

Ever since she'd been able to hold up a hairbrush to use as a substitute microphone, she'd been singing along in her room to the latest hits on the radio. She supposed she'd inherited the love of singing from her father, who was always belting out Waylon Jennings truckie songs in his rig. She'd even managed to score a few singing lessons from a teacher at one of the schools she'd been to, who'd urged her to continue training and develop her voice professionally when she left.

And it wasn't just singing that she loved. She was into writing songs as well. She'd spent plenty of nights before she'd left home tucked away in her room with a battered old guitar – the latest argument she'd had with her mother still ringing in her ears – writing songs that tried to show how she felt about the world. It was as though the music allowed her to express herself in a way that straight talking never would.

She kept the quieter, more complex songs she wrote very private – she wasn't really ready yet to share them with anyone. The raps were different. Raps were meant to be shared with people. She'd really enjoyed getting up and showing the kids at Hartley High what she was made of, and in a way she'd never thought possible, it had paid off. Kids like Rose and

Danielle, who'd been initially stand-offish, were now her friends. Maybe not close friends yet, but close enough. Jodie didn't like people getting too close to her.

What she had liked, though, was the audience, being the centre of attention, having the kids in the playground listening and dancing to her music. It had been even better at the Valentine's Day dance. She'd really only made up the Valentine rap as she went along – Nick had dragged her over to the mike and made her do it. But once she'd started, she hadn't wanted to stop. The words and rhymes had just kept on flowing. From that night on she'd been sure about what she wanted to do with her life: become a professional musician.

So when she'd met a guy at her sister's friend's party last week who'd said he was an executive from a record company, she knew she just had to take a chance and introduce herself. She'd waltzed him into a corner, stocked him up with a never-ending supply of drinks and crisps, and done the hard sell on him about her song-writing abilities. She couldn't believe he'd actually agreed to give her a chance. Well, to be honest, it had been more along the lines of "get a demo tape together and I'll have a listen", but at least she had a name and face to put to a phone number now. Hopefully he'd remember hers.

And now she had less than two days to do it in. She had a hunch the offer wasn't going to be around for ever. It was important to get in while he still vaguely remembered who she was. The poor guy must meet a zillion hopefuls a week! Brian had agreed to help her put the demo together. He'd programmed an excellent backing on the drum machine, and added in a few special effects from the synth. Things had been looking really good – until the amp decided to chuck a wobbly.

Brian gave one last twiddle. 'Okay, Jodie,' he said, 'let's give it another try.' He fired up the drum machine and played the opening chords on his guitar.

Jodie started singing. Maybe, this time ...

Con barged into the room, looking for Nick. The amplifier suddenly went berko, squealing in protest. Jodie's nose wrinkled. What was that smell?

'Brian!' she gasped. 'Check out the amp. It's having a heart attack.'

Brian looked over at the wisps of smoke pluming from the back of the ancient Marshall. 'Valve's burnt out,' he said. 'Probably too much overload on the power circuit.' He gave the amp a pat. 'Looks like the poor old fella's finally carked it,' he sighed.

'Oh, great!' said Jodie. 'Now what?'

Con cut her off. 'Nick, mate! I've been looking all over for you.'

'So you found me,' said Nick. 'Where's the fire?'

Jodie smirked.

'C'mon, Nick,' insisted Con. 'We've got practice. The soccer final. What are you hanging around in here for?'

Nick was torn. He knew he should have been at practice by now. This final was really important. But Jodie looked like she needed him.

Jodie studied the back of the amp with Brian. 'So can you fix it?' she asked.

Brian shook his head. 'It's cactus, mate.'

'Oh, great,' said Jodie. She turned to Nick. 'What am I going to do? Without the amp, I can't make a tape. And without the tape ...' She shrugged her shoulders. 'I guess I'm going to miss out on my big chance.'

Nick moved towards her, ignoring Con. 'Ah ... is there anything I can do?'

Jodie shrugged her shoulders in defeat. 'Not unless you've got a fairy godmother. Without an amp ...'

'I'll get you an amp,' said Nick.

Jodie stared at him, amazed. 'How?'

Nick grinned. 'Trust me.'

Jodie gave him a look that would melt a construction worker's hard hat. 'You can really get me an amp?' she asked.

Nick grinned back at her. He hadn't the faintest idea *how* he was going to get Jodie an amp, but he'd find a way somehow. For Jodie, he'd go to the moon.

Jodie tenderly traced the outline of his cheek with her fingertips. 'What did I ever do without you?' she whispered. She zipped her mike into its case. 'Check you later, Brian,' she called back over her shoulder, as she left the room.

Nick turned back to Con, eyes shining. 'Did you hear that, mate? "What did she ever do without me." I think maybe she's falling for me. What do you reckon?'

Con slammed the soccer ball he was holding into Nick's stomach. 'The final, is what I reckon.'

Nick grabbed the ball from Con and began to spin it on his hand. 'Geez, Con, how am I ever going to get an amp?'

'Forget the amp,' said Con. 'Think goals, lots of goals. You're my main man, remember.'

Nick looked at Con speculatively. 'You want goals, no worries. But, listen. I get you a a goal, you get me an amp.'

Con stared at him. 'Are you serious? How am I going to get an amp?'

Nick pushed him out the door and down the corridor. 'Because,' he said, applying a wrestling hold to his arm, 'you're my main man ... '

It had taken a few phone calls, but Con had finally managed to track down an amp for Nick. His uncle Stavros, who managed a Greek reception centre, had confirmed that yes, he did indeed have an amplifier on the premises. Unfortunately, Con had neglected to mention that he intended taking it away.

Con's Buick, with Nick and Jodie aboard, screamed into the parking lot of the Adelphi Reception Centre with a squeal of tyres. The three jumped out and threaded their way through a maze of poker machines, looking for Con's uncle. Jodie winced at the bouzouki music playing discreetly in the background.

When they finally caught up with Stavros, he was less than amused. 'Con, all I said to you on the phone was that I had an amplifier. I didn't make you any promises. Give me one good reason why I should lend it to you?'

Con plucked at his stripy T-shirt. 'Hey, man, I'm family.'

His uncle looked down at his precious amp – a top of the range Peavey – and across to Jodie. 'Family, uh,' he sighed. 'I ask this bum to help out at my daughter Melina's engagement party. Park the cars. And what do I find? He's put a sign up saying "Valet Parking, Five Bucks". I ask you . . . '

Jodie smiled. 'I hope it was a nice party.'

'Are you kidding?' Stavros sneered. 'She split with the creep two days later.' He turned his attention to Nick. 'So, tell me, why do you want to borrow my amp, anyway? Some sort of concert, is it?'

Con jumped in before Nick could blow it. 'That's right, Uncle Stavros. A concert, for charity.'

'Charity, uh,' said his uncle, suddenly suspicious. 'What kind of charity?'

'It's for little dudes, Uncle Stavros. Orphans,' said Con, rapidly improvising.

Jodie looked at Con's uncle's face. By the expression on it, things weren't looking good. She decided to try to speed things up a bit by painting a picture even the Scroogiest of reception centre-managing uncles couldn't be moved by. 'Mr Georgiou? Hi, I'm Jodie. I sing a bit, you see, in a band. And we're ... we're trying to raise enough money to give these poor kids some kind of Christmas holiday ...' She looked across at Nick and Con, who nodded encouragingly. 'By the sea,' she added.

Con's uncle looked at her thoughtfully. 'Are you with him?' he asked, jerking his thumb at his nephew.

Jodie looked affronted. 'With Con? No way!'

Mr Georgiou nodded his shiny, bald head. 'Thank God for that,' he said. 'It's been nice meeting you, Jodie, you're an angel. Come on inside and get the amp.'

The three exchanged looks of relief as they followed him up the stairs into the equipment room. Mr Georgiou started to push the amp towards Nick and Con, then stopped. 'I got a wedding here tomorrow night,' he said, cracking his knuckles. 'I want it back, you hear me? In one piece.'

Con smiled his cheesiest smile. 'Not a problem, Unc.'

'It better not be,' answered his uncle, his voice like doom. 'Because if I don't get this amp back tomorrow, you are seriously going to wish you'd never been born. Understand?'

Con nodded mutely. Uncle Stavros was one member of the family you *definitely* didn't mess with.

Chapter Eight

Get it down, play it out
Baby when you feel so lonely ...

Jodie's strong vocals reverberated round the music room. Nick, watching from the corner, was rapt. Both the song and the amp sounded great! And it was all down to him. Now if this didn't win him points with Jodie, nothing would.

Brian strummed the final chords on his Fender. 'You're amazing, Nick,' he said. 'You actually got us a piece of equipment that works.'

Nick grinned. 'What did you expect? This thing's designed to survive Greek weddings.'

'Yeah,' joked Brian, 'I can see the white marks where they smashed the plates on it. You ready to put the track down now, Jodie?'

Jodie nodded. The song was sounding great. She'd really have something to show the A&R guy from the record company. She was just getting ready to start recording when Mr Brown, the music teacher, poked his head into the room.

'Sorry, guys,' he said. 'Time to pack up.'

'But we've only just started, sir,' cried Jodie in alarm.

Mr Brown was apologetic. 'Look guys, I'm sorry, but I've got to lock up. The cleaners will be around soon. Ten minutes, okay?' He smiled at Jodie. 'That song sounded hot, Jodie. Well done.' He headed off down the corridor, jangling his keys.

Jodie smiled, frustrated to be losing valuable recording time, but happy all the same. If Mr Brown thought it was good . . .

Brian had other ideas. 'Geez, don't tell me the teachers like the music. That's the kiss of death.'

Nick laughed and tugged Jodie's hair. 'You coming to Ruby's?'

Jodie smiled up at him. 'Sure.' She gave him a hug, then turned back to Brian. 'You can pack up, can't you, Brian?'

Brian watched Nick and Jodie disappear down the corridor, giggling and flirting like third-formers. He sighed, then began the long, slow process of rolling up and checking the leads.

Ruby's was jumping by the time Nick and Jodie arrived. The pool tables were full, with people queueing up to play, quietly moving to the acid jazz oozing from the speakers. Ruby herself was doing a roaring trade in drinks and snacks.

Nick picked up two milk-shakes from the counter and squeezed into a corner booth beside Jodie, who was in a dangerously flirtatious mood. He chuckled as she dangled her straw in her milk-shake, then fed drops of it, bit by bit, into his mouth like he was a baby. Every now and then she stopped to give him a big, wet, milk-shakey kiss.

Rose and Chaka, playing pool in the opposite corner, put down their cues and watched.

Rose watched Nick stick the tongue in. 'So you reckon they're doing it, or what?' she asked Chaka.

Chaka shrugged. 'Looks pretty serious to me.'

Con wandered in, and noticing Nick, hurried over, burbling on about the upcoming soccer final. Without taking his eyes off Jodie, Nick fished in his pocket for a dollar coin, and held it out to Con.

'Here, mate. Take this and go and play some pool.'

'You gonna play too, Nick . . . ?' began Con, not quite picking up on the signals Nick was silently sending him. Then it suddenly clicked. He wandered over to join Chaka and Rose, unable to believe his luck. A free game!

Free of any interruptions, Nick returned to the task at hand – sucking face with Jodie.

Rose potted the black and looked up to find the gruesome twosome still at it. 'Wow . . . ' she breathed. 'That's some session. So, *are* they, or aren't they?'

Con gawped. 'Dunno. Maybe. They don't waste much time, eh.' Chuckling, he inserted the dollar coin in the slot, and watched the balls come crashing down. He wondered what Nick's movements were likely to be for the rest of the evening. Not playing pool, that was for sure!

Nick walked Jodie home through the darkening streets, his arm draped around her shoulders. 'Just as well I've got you round to protect me,' said Jodie, giving him a squeeze. 'This area's the pits at night.'

Nick stopped suddenly and drew her close. 'You think I'd let anything happen to you?' he asked, tracing his fingers along her cheek. He kissed her.

Jodie slid her fingers round to the back of his neck, tracing his collar with little feathery movements. Nick shivered. God, that felt good. Their kiss grew more passionate.

A blood-curdling yowl followed by a thump and clatter interrupted them before either of them could get too carried away. 'Jesus!' said Nick. 'What was that?'

Jodie laughed. 'Only a cat. Out for a good time and missing out. It's probably jealous.' She gently stroked Nick's stomach. 'With good reason.'

They walked on around the corner till they came to Jodie's apartment building.

'Are you going to ask me in?' asked Nick, pulling her close again.

Jodie pulled away. 'Lights are on. That means Linda's home. We wouldn't have ... I don't ... I just don't think it's a good idea.' She kissed him lightly on the bridge of his nose. 'I'll see you at school tomorrow, okay?'

'Just try and stop me,' said Nick, framing her face with his hands. 'Room 27. Nine o'clock.'

'You got it,' said Jodie. She kissed him again, then ran up the stairs and into her flat, abandoning Nick to the cats and the night.

Con watched Danielle giving Steve major grief. When were those two going to get their act together, he wondered? They'd been an item since about halfway through Year 10, and he didn't think he'd ever seen them get through a whole week without some kind of argument. Today's flare-up seemed to be about Danielle playing soccer. Con wasn't too sure exactly how he felt about a chick playing soccer, but hey, if she wanted to play, and she could cut it with the guys ... well, that was fine by him. Maybe Steve was jealous of the other guys paying her attention when she helped win matches. Who knew?

Besides, he had more pressing matters on his mind. His cousin, Nick. If the guy had scored, he wanted to be the first to know. After all, he was family, wasn't he? These things were important in families.

He saw Nick come out of the toilet block and waved him over. 'So, Nick, you went out last night, uh? After Ruby's?'

Nick bounced the ball he was carrying off his foot. He looked sideways at Con. 'Yeah. So what?'

Con moved in close. 'With Jodie, mate?' He tapped his nose. 'You and Jodie?'

'Mind your own business!' Nick snapped.

Con noticed he was blushing. 'You have a good time, mate?'

'Are you deaf as well as dumb?' said Nick, but Con could see he was weakening. Well, he was smiling, anyway. That was a good sign he was about to spill the beans.

He moved in for the kill, keeping up an endless barrage of questions. 'So what did ya do, man? Did ya do it? Did ya? You can tell me, man, I'm your cousin.'

He checked Nick's face. He was grinning broadly now. Paydirt! 'Ya did, didn't ya! Ya did it with her!' He punched Nick on the arm. 'You're a tiger, man, a tiger.'

Nick swatted Con away, as though he was a particularly pesky mosquito. He threw him the ball. 'So are we gonna play soccer, or what?' he asked, running on ahead.

The bell signalling the end of period four rang. Con and Steve shouldered their way out into the corridor, pleased to be finished with another morning's school.

'Hey Steve,' said Con, 'when are you and Danni going to finally get it together?'

Steve sighed. 'Who knows, man. She's always nagging me about something or other. And she never listens to me. Now take this soccer thing ...'

He was interrupted by Nick jumping on him from behind. 'Gee, was that lesson boring or what,' he said, throwing Steve some mock punches.

'Hey, Nicky boy,' said Con, joining in the fun, 'where do you get all that energy from? Shouldn't you be saving it for later, Superstud?'

Steve stared at Con. 'What's all this Superstud crap?' he asked.

Con leaned in close to Steve. 'If you see a big smile on Jodie's face, it ain't because she's been watching Bart Simpson, man.'

Steve was impressed. 'You nailed her?' he asked Nick.

Nick grinned sheepishly.

'All right!' said Steve, punching the air. He dropped his voice. 'How was it?'

But Nick had had enough. 'Drop it, okay,' he warned.

Steve, unfazed, gave him a few man-to-man punches to the stomach. 'Way to go, Nick!' he called, before scooting off down the corridor, in search of an audience.

Nick turned to Con, still flushed. 'Can't you keep your big mouth shut?' he asked.

Con blinked at him. So what had he done wrong this time?

Over at the gym, Danielle and the girls were getting into shape. Decked out in aerobic tights and leotards, they skipped rope, did endless stomach crunches and pumped iron. Danielle's eyes were brimming with mischief. She'd just dropped a bomb-shell about Nick's and Jodie's extra-curricular activities and Rose and Chaka were lapping it up.

'So who did you hear it from?' asked Rose.

'Janey,' said Danielle, flexing her abdominal muscles.

'Steve told Janey . . . and Nick told Steve.'

Rose looked doubtful. 'What do you reckon?'

Danielle grunted as she picked up the weights. 'I wouldn't believe anything Steve told me.'

'Yeah, but hey, you were at Ruby's yesterday,' pointed out Rose. 'You saw them. Nick was all over her like a rash. Tongue samba time.' She gagged.

'So who did you hear it from?' Chaka asked Rose.

'Rivers,' said Rose. 'As per usual, he was telling all his mates. Loudly,' she sniggered.

'So it's all over the school?' asked Chaka. She broke off as Jodie walked in and slung her gym bag in the corner.

'What's the problem?' Jodie asked Chaka.

Chaka shrugged. 'No problem.'

'So why have you guys been ignoring me all morning?' asked Jodie, her eyes popping. 'Come on, admit it. You've been ignoring me.'

'Ask her, Danielle,' whispered Rose, fiercely.

'No, you ask her,' Danielle whispered back.

Jodie gave them the full-on glare treatment.

'Are you and Nick together?' asked Danielle.

Jodie rolled her eyes. 'Together?'

'You know, together,' said Danielle, struggling to put it delicately enough.

'You know,' put in Chaka, helpfully, 'an item.'

'An item?' asked Jodie. She was really lost now.

Rose came to the rescue. 'You know, are you doing it with him.'

78

The gym suddenly went silent. Jodie's face went through the full complement of shades of the spectrum. 'What!' she roared, finally.

'Are ... you doing it with him?' asked Rose, less confidently this time.

'Where do you get off asking me that sort of question?' spat Jodie, her stomach suddenly doing backflips.

'Well, it's just that the rest of the school thinks you are,' said Danielle, sheepishly. 'There's rumours all over the place.'

'Has Nick been saying it?' demanded Jodie. 'Has he?'

Danielle wished she'd never opened her big mouth. 'Steve said he got it from Nick,' she said reluctantly.

Jodie's face crumpled for a moment, then flushed red with rage. The bastard!

'Hey,' said Chaka, feeling a little guilty for helping spread the gossip. 'Guys can be pigs sometimes, but I wouldn't peak over it.'

Jodie picked up her gym bag and headed for the door. 'I can't believe it,' she muttered.

Rose and Chaka called her back, but she was off, ready to wage war on anything Greek she might come across in the corridor.

'Oops,' said Chaka, picking up the medicine ball.

Jodie cornered Nick in the Humanities wing and hustled him into the Geography room before he had a chance to know what had hit him.

'Have you been telling people I slept with you?' she demanded, her eyes dripping sparks.

Nick put his arms up in appeal. 'Me? No way ...'

Jodie slapped them down again. 'Then why are people saying it?'

Nick stalled for time. 'Come on ... who?'

'Steve said it,' snapped Jodie.

'I can't help what Steve thinks,' reasoned Nick.

'Did he ask you?'

Nick looked at the door, the window, the posters on the wall – anywhere but at her face.

Jodie's shoulders dropped. She let out a long, angry, breath. 'I thought so.'

Nick, realising she was about to walk out on him, grabbed her arm. 'Look, wait a minute ...'

'Get your hands off me!' Jodie shrieked.

'I never said we were doing anything,' said Nick, desperately.

Jodie looked at Nick for a moment, taking in the smooth features, the expressive eyes, the well-shaped mouth. She'd thought maybe this one was going to be a little different from all the rest, but he'd turned out to be just the same. Interested in only one thing: himself. Why was it that guys always let their egos get in the way of their nicer qualities? Well, she wasn't going to hang around with this one any more to find out. As far as she was concerned, he was history.

She kept her voice even. 'So you didn't tell them we were doing anything. So what? You didn't tell them that we weren't either, did you? You just let them believe it. Made you feel like a real hero, didn't it.'

Nick blushed.

Jodie turned the screw a little deeper. 'Well, thanks a lot, Nick,' she said. 'So much for my reputation.' Holding her head high, she sauntered off down the corridor, leaving Nick alone to deal with his angst.

Chapter Nine

Nick was mortified. What had he done? Just when it looked like he was finally getting through to Jodie, he'd blown it. Like totally. She was never going to forgive him now. And when he thought about it, he couldn't really blame her.

Her parting words, about how he was only interested in himself, hung in the air like Sydney smog. The worst part about them was that they just weren't true. He thought a lot about Jodie, and not just about how to get her into bed either. It was kind of weird. He hadn't really felt like this about any other girl before. Not even Martina, the hot chick he'd had a crush on when he was in Year 8. No – Jodie was different. Serious stuff.

But he had his reputation with the guys to think of, as well. All that macho male-bonding locker-room stuff everyone was into these days. He guessed that was why he hadn't come clean about things when Con had been hassling him for details. Jesus! Life was just too hard sometimes.

He held Steve partly responsible for what had happened. Well, that's where Jodie said she had heard it from, though how Steve knew anything was beyond him. Steve. Mr Big Mouth, eh? Well, maybe it was about time he put his big mouth into action and helped get him out of this mess. Somebody had to. Jodie didn't seem like the type of girl who gave people second chances without major persuasion.

He wandered over to the canteen. Maybe a 'roll in a roll' would help settle his stomach. It felt like the tanks from Tiananmen Square were rolling through it at the moment. He saw Steve buying a Mars Bar, and swooped on him.

'Sure your mouth's big enough to fit that in?' he asked him.

'Whuh . . . ?' said Steve.

'I oughta break your face,' snarled Nick.

Steve looked confused. 'What did I ever do to you?'

'Where do you get off telling people I've been doing it with Jodie?' Nick demanded.

'Hey, cool it, would you,' said Steve, looking nervously around him. 'Con was doing all the talking. Anyway, I didn't think it was any big secret.'

Nick paused for a moment. 'Con, eh . . . ?' he said. Well, at least that made a bit more sense. When it came to big mouths, Con's was like the entrance to Luna Park.

Now that the pressure was off him, Steve wasn't one to miss an opportunity. 'So, like, what are you saying, Nick . . . did you nail her, or what?'

It was a mistake. Nick turned on him savagely. 'I'm saying, the next person who says anything about me and Jodie, I'm going to put 'em in Casualty!'

Steve's health was saved by the arrival of Con, the master-mouth himself. Seeing a chance for escape from an imminent face-rearrangement, Steve muttered something about meeting Danielle, and discreetly snuck away.

Now it was Con's turn for a blasting. 'You've been telling people me and Jodie are sleeping together.'

'Yeah, mate. So what?'

'So now she hates my guts, mate.'

Con looked genuinely shocked. 'You mean, it's not true now?'

Nick looked down, embarrassed. 'It never even happened,' he muttered.

'Man, you know me, mate?' said Con, his honour wounded. 'I wouldn't have said anything if I didn't think it was true. Why didn't you set me straight?'

Nick flushed a little. Con was probably right. But that still didn't let him off the hook. 'Look, Jodie's really humiliated, and you've got to fix it.'

Con looked affronted. 'Me? Right. And how am I going to do that?'

The bell rang. Nick slapped Con on the back, then headed off to his locker. As far as he was concerned, he'd passed the problem on to his cousin. 'You'll think of something,' he called back cheerfully. 'You always do.'

The last class of the day was English with Ms Milano. Steve and Danielle seemed to have patched up their latest drama. They entered the room wrapped around each other like wrestling anacondas.

'And so you really forgive me?' asked Steve, nibbling Danielle's ear lobe.

'Keep that up for the next fifty years and I'll think about it,' said Danielle, sliding her hands round his neck. She pulled his face down and settled down to some serious snogging, causing the rest of the class to break into hoots and cheers. They were used to Steve and Danielle's 'breaking and making up' sessions by now.

Ms Milano came into the room and went straight to the blackboard, a list of questions in her hand. She tapped Steve on the shoulder as she brushed past. 'Would it be too much trouble to keep sex out of my classroom?' she asked lightly.

Ms Milano pulled the cord on the map blind which had been left unrolled, and sent it rocketing towards the top of the blackboard. The class broke up. Behind it, somebody had scrawled in huge chalky letters: 'I GOT IT WRONG. JODIE IS NOT DOING IT WITH NICK.'

Ms Milano gasped. Jodie blanched. Nick felt like he was going to pass out.

'Make up your mind, Jodie,' called the ever-vigilant Rivers from the back of the room. 'Who *are* you doing it with?'

Jodie fired one of her slater-killing looks over at Nick, who wished the floor would open up and swallow him. If things had been bad before, they were his worst nightmare now. He wondered how much it would cost to emigrate to South America.

Ms Milano was less than amused. 'Whoever did this can come up here and wipe it off. What, no volunteers?'

She scanned her class's faces slowly, looking for a twinge of guilty conscience. She tapped the board. 'This is not a very funny joke. So whoever did it obviously has no sense of humour ... and no courage.'

Finally, Con levered himself out from his desk and stood up, his face as sad as a wet Saturday. The class went berserk.

'It's not a joke, Miss,' he announced sorrowfully. 'It was meant to be an apology.'

His teacher shot him a serious look. 'I'm not going to ask what all this is about, Con. But if you want to apologise to someone, I'd say the best way to do it is face to face.'

Con's face grew even sadder. He shuffled over to Jodie's desk. 'Jodie . . . ?' he began. She raised her chin. 'Jodie, I . . . I'm sorry. I've behaved like a jerk. A jerk with a big mouth.' He looked down at his chalky fingers. 'And stupid ideas.'

Jodie allowed herself to crack the slightest of smiles.

'Jodie,' said Con, looking her straight in the eye, 'I apologise for insulting you.'

The class broke up again. Rose, Chaka and some of the other girls applauded.

Jodie looked at Con. She supposed the poor guy had suffered enough. At least the dork had apologised. She glanced over at Nick, expecting to see him gloating. She wouldn't have been surprised to know he'd been behind all this . . .

It was as though he'd read her mind. He raised his eyebrows and shrugged, indicating he'd known nothing about the whole deal. Jodie allowed him the briefest of smiles. She wasn't letting him off the hook just quite yet.

Knowing that Jodie had another recording session after school, Nick followed her to the music room as soon as the final bell rang. He put on his meekest hangdog expression and hung about in the corner while she and Brian set up, waiting for Jodie to throw him a conciliatory bone. He didn't have to wait for long.

'Just admit it, Nick,' said Jodie, plugging in her microphone and checking the levels. 'You put Con up to it.'

Nick pounced on his chance. 'No, I didn't. I told him to set things straight, that's all.'

Jodie adjusted a slider, her back to Nick. 'It was a dumb thing to do in the first place.'

Nick moved closer to her. 'Well, I was just being selfish. I wasn't . . . thinking about you. I'm sorry.'

Nick stroked her shoulder, coaxing her to face him. 'What makes me mad is that I never even realised that it was going to hurt you.' He pulled her closer. 'I would never do anything to hurt you.'

Jodie gave him a brief smile, then brushed his cheek with her lips. 'Repeat after me,' she whispered. 'I am a dork.'

'You are a dork,' whispered Nick, then yelped as her fingers dug into his rib-cage.

Jodie pulled away and looked anxiously over at Brian, who was busily making himself scarce, fiddling about with the four-track.

'You better go,' she said to Nick. 'This is it. My last chance to get the demo done. I have to drop it in to that guy tomorrow.' She squeezed his hand, her face pale. 'I'll talk to you later.'

Nick picked up on her mood. 'Hey, don't be nervous,' he said, returning the squeeze. 'You'll be great. You *are* great.'

'Thanks,' said Jodie, meaning it.

Nick was halfway out the door when Con rushed in, waving his mobile at them. 'I'm sorry, guys,' he said, starting to unhook the leads from the amp, 'I gotta pull the plug.'

'What!' spluttered Nick.

'Uncle Stavros wants the amp back. Now! I can't stall him, either. He's already on his way.'

Jodie shot Nick a panic-stricken look. Nick jumped in to save her.

'Con, if Jodie doesn't do this recording session now, this afternoon, she's going to lose her chance. These A&R guys don't hang around for ever, you know.' He grabbed the lead back from Con. 'The amp stays,' he said firmly.

Con shrugged. 'Well ... tell her to sing faster! Because the last guy who tried to put one over on Uncle Stavros ... trust me, you don't wanna know what he did to him.'

Nick winced. 'And you say he's coming now? Couldn't you have given him a bum steer? Told him the wrong school or something?'

'He's my uncle!' said Con, surprised Nick could be so stupid.

Nick looked around the room for inspiration. When none came, he mentally started repacking his bags for South America. He was going to need an escape route if Jodie missed out on this record deal because of him.

Brian picked up his guitar. 'Look, why don't we just start anyway? Maybe this guy will get held up in traffic or something.'

'Good idea,' said Jodie. She pushed Con out into the corridor. 'You wait out there for your uncle, Con, and if he turns up, let Nick know and he can warn us.' She grabbed her mike. 'Let's go, Brian.'

Brian fired up the drum machine and four-track and launched into the opening chords on his guitar. Nick stayed in the room just long enough to hear Jodie sing the opening verse, then moved to the other side of the door, guarding it with his life. Moments later, Con's woolly head, held in an armlock, appeared around the corner. Nick gulped. Uncle Stavros ...

He rushed over to welcome him. 'Mr Georgiou! How you doing? Come to check out your fave nephew's place of learning, did you?'

Stavros glared at him, gold teeth glinting. 'I think I'm being done,' he said, applying a tad more pressure to Con's neck.

'Unc ... you see, it's like this ... ' stammered Con.

His uncle swatted his excuses away. 'Shuddup!' He turned

to Nick. 'I don't see no orphans,' he said. 'No orphans, and no concerts. Did he sell my amp?'

'No . . .' Nick began.

'Lucky for you,' said Stavros, twisting Con's neck. The trio reached the music room door. Even with the soundproofing, Jodie's strong vocals could be heard easily.

'It's actually in here,' said Nick. He put his hand up as Stavros attempted to push his way in. 'But you can't go in now . . . they're recording!'

Stavros slapped Nick's hand away, his muscles bulging. 'Not for long,' he said.

Nick threw himself in front of the door. 'Jodie's in there . . . remember?' He flapped his arms. 'The little angel?'

'The one who's not with me,' Con reminded him, rubbing his neck now that he'd finally been released.

Nick went into full-on violins and roses mode. 'Her whole future hangs on this tape she's making. If you stop it now, she won't get another chance.'

Stavros looked down at him. 'Nick . . . you touch my heart. You really do.' He reached for the door handle again. 'But, tough cookies, I need the amp . . .'

Nick barred his way yet again. 'You could always hire another amp for the wedding,' he pleaded.

Stavros laughed. 'Why should I spend my money?'

Nick's brain ticked over, scrabbling for solutions. 'All right, *we'll* pay for it.' He glanced sideways at Con.

'Yeah!' confirmed Con.

Stavros peered through the window at Jodie belting out her song. Noticing what was going on outside the door, she rolled her eyes and winked at him. Stavros cleared his throat. 'Her future, you say?'

'Right!' said Nick and Con as one, fingers crossed behind their backs.

Stavros took one last look through the window, then turned back to his nephew. He scratched his shiny head. 'I tell you what . . .' he began.

Nick let out a long sigh of relief. Everything was going to be okay.

Okay, so there were definitions and definitions of okay, thought Nick, as he plunged his arms once more into a greasy sink full of thick, white plates. Greek bouzouki music filled the air, wafting in from the banquet hall next door. He reckoned if he saw another slice of baklava he'd throw up.

' "I can get you an amp, Nick",' he trilled sarcastically to Con, who was scraping taramasalata from serving dishes.

'Just remember,' said Con, waving a knife at him, 'I'm doing this for your girlfriend.'

'Yeah,' said Nick, sloshing the water about moodily. 'Probably my ex-girlfriend now. How many courses to go?'

'Are you kidding?' asked Con. 'This is a Greek wedding! Hey, Jodie!' he called, as she danced into the room, waving a cassette tape.

Jodie looked around at the mountains of crockery and laughed. 'Maybe you should smash a few more,' she said. 'It would be less to wash. So how are you guys doing?'

Nick peeled off his pink rubber gloves and threw them on the draining board. He gestured to the cassette. 'So, did it work or what?' he asked.

Jodie shot him a coy look. 'Well, I'm rapt, but I want you guys to have a listen,' she said, modestly.

Nick exhanged the tape for the one in the kitchen ghetto

blaster, and hit the play button. Jodie's song reverberated around the kitchen walls. Waiting staff, on their way out to the banquet hall with more dishes, came back into the kitchen. 'Hey, that's great!' said Con's cousin Despina, grabbing Con and pulling him into the centre of the room to dance.

Jodie and Nick watched as one by one, the rest of the kitchen staff joined in. 'So you think it's really good?' Jodie asked Nick, moving in close.

'Really, really, *really* good,' whispered Nick, his lips brushing hers. He gave her waist a light squeeze, then got down to business. South America was starting to look *very* much like a second option ...

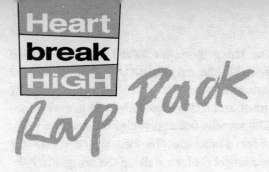

Chapter Ten

Con's car, speakers blaring Jodie's demo tape, screeched to a stop in the foreshore carpark. Nick and Jodie and the rest of the gang, who'd been piled into the back seat, spilled out onto the road.

'Hey, check out the waves, man!' called Con to Steve. 'Race you in.'

Steve grabbed his towel and dashed down the wooden stairs, only seconds behind Con. Dodging little kids building sand-castles, and serious sun-worshippers stretched out on towels, they threw themselves headlong into the water. The rest of the crew made their way down at a more leisurely pace.

'Your tape sounds good, Jodie,' said Jack.

Jodie smiled. 'Yeah, it's mad, isn't it! Brian's done a great job. Let's just hope the record company guy likes it too.' She stopped to watch a couple of surfers glide effortlessly into shore on the curl of a wave. Hopefully her intro into the music scene would be that smooth.

She laughed as Rose and Chaka each grabbed one of Jack's hands and pulled him down the stairs and across the sand. It was good to see him getting out a bit and mixing in with the other kids. Seems like she and Jack had both made some good friends in the past few weeks.

Nick slid his arm around her waist. 'Hey, looks like everyone's having a good time. Was this a great idea of mine or what?'

Jodie threw him a quick kiss. 'The best. Why don't we lose the crowd for a while? Go for a walk up the beach a bit?'

Nick watched Danielle dunking Steve. 'What, and miss all the fun?' Jodie glared at him. 'Only kidding,' he whispered, pulling her in close and nibbling her ear. 'I'd follow you anywhere.'

Jodie pointed to a pile of rocks further up the beach. 'Let's go up there,' she said. 'It looks kind of ... private.'

Nick rolled over and checked his watch. Six o'clock. Getting on for going-home time. Not that he wanted to ... the sun was still really warm on his skin. He lay there for another few minutes, listening to the waves crashing onto the sand. Then, pulling himself up onto his elbow, he gazed down at Jodie, her eyes closed against the sun.

'You are *so* beautiful,' he whispered, his finger tracing the curve of her cheek. Jodie opened one eye.

'I bet you say that to all the girls,' she said, closing it again.

Nick grinned. 'Only the beautiful ones.'

'Oh, yeah?' said Jodie, starting to take an interest. 'And how many *beautiful* ones have there been?'

Nick squirmed slightly, suddenly shy. This stuff wasn't easy to talk about. Not to someone he cared so much for, anyway. 'Well, I'm not a virgin, if that's what you mean,' he said finally.

'I didn't think so somehow,' said Jodie. She looked across at a white bird, slowly coming in to land.

Nick picked up a pile of sand, and let the grains trickle out between his fingers. 'How about you?' asked Nick.

'I've slept with two guys,' said Jodie.

'Did you love them?'

'I thought I did at the time. But it didn't last ... we just drifted apart.'

'So what about us?' asked Nick, slowly. He took her hand. 'I love you, you know?'

'I love you too,' she said, kissing him, then pulling away. There was more she needed to know. 'So what about your love life?'

Nick cleared his throat. 'Nothing much to tell, really.'

Jodie rolled her eyes. 'Oh yeah? I know you're not so modest with Con and the guys.'

Nick flushed. 'Yeah, well ... the truth is there's been a couple for me too.'

'Oh, yeah? Only a couple?' said Jodie, grabbing his waist. 'A guy like you? Sure.'

Nick yelped. 'Hey! Quit tickling me!' He grabbed her arms, pinning them behind her back. They mock-wrestled for a while, then collapsed in a heap, giggling. Jodie looked back down the beach where the rest of the gang were gathered. Steve and Danielle were standing at the water's edge, engaged in a tonsil tango. She leaned towards Nick. 'My sister's working all night tonight,' she whispered.

Nick grinned. 'That's a shame ...' he said, picking up some sand and tossing it at Jodie. 'For her!'

Jodie opened her apartment door and flicked on the lights. 'You home, Linda?' she called softly. She waited a moment for a reply, then turned to Nick. 'Looks like we're on our own ...'

She moved ahead of him into the room, picking up magazines, straightening cushions, looking everywhere but at Nick. He sat down on the edge of the sofa, and began shredding the label of a wine bottle on the coffee table. 'Umm ...' he began, then stopped. 'Nice place you got here, Jodie.'

Jodie looked around at the rickety furniture – second-hand, most of it, from op shops. But there were splashes of colour everywhere – posters on the walls, flowers and candles on the benchtops. 'It's home, I guess,' she said. She moved towards Nick, then away again. He stood up, drawing her close, his lips on her neck.

Jodie shivered. 'I've got salt everywhere,' she whispered into his chest.

'You're still beautiful,' said Nick, moving his mouth to her shoulder.

Jodie pulled away, her green eyes glinting with mischief. 'Umm ... I think I'll take a shower,' she announced, slithering off towards the bathroom. The door closed behind her.

Nick watched her disappear. Now what? His mind raced. He sat down on the sofa again, wondering what he was supposed to do next.

He didn't have to wonder for long. The bathroom door creaked slowly open again. Jodie appeared, wrapped in a towel, her wispy blonde hair hanging loosely around her face.

'Ah ... haven't you got salt on you too?' she asked coyly, before disappearing once again.

Nick turned off the taps and turned towards Jodie, water streaming from his hair and face. 'Got a towel for me?' he asked.

'You can share mine,' she laughed, moving in close and

94

folding the ends around his back. He brushed the wet fronds of hair out of her eyes, then hugged her.

Jodie licked his neck. 'Much better without salt,' she whispered. 'Did you come prepared?'

'Whuh?' asked Nick. Now what was she on about?

Jodie rolled her eyes. 'Condoms, stupid.'

Nick blushed. How could he have been so dumb? 'Yeah, sure,' he stammered.

Jodie smiled, letting the towel slip to the floor. She moved towards the bedroom, holding out her hand. 'Coming?' she asked.

Nick grinned. Sliding his arm under her knees, he picked Jodie up and carried her into the bedroom, where he dumped her, laughing, in the middle of the double bed. 'Waddya reckon?' he asked, sliding onto the bed beside her.

Jodie rolled over on top of him, pinning his arms with her hands. 'Just shut up and kiss me.'

Mrs Poulos was beside herself with worry. One o'clock in the morning and still no sign of Nick. She reached for the phone. 'I'm calling the police!' she called to her husband.

George Poulos grabbed the phone back from her. 'And what are you going to say? He's eighteen years old and he's a few hours late?'

'He's very late,' wailed his wife.

'Look, he's all right. I'm sure of it. He'll be out with the boys somewhere.'

'He could be hurt ... dead in the gutter somewhere!' continued Mrs Poulos.

'He's going to wish he was by the time I'm finished with him,' ranted her husband. He handed her the phone again.

'Why don't you call your sister. See if he's over there with Con.'

Mrs Poulos sniffed away her tears of worry, and made the call. She spoke rapidly in Greek for a few minutes, then turned to her husband, her eyes huge. 'He's not there. Con's there. He's been there for hours ... asleep.' Her voice rose a pitch. 'So where is he?'

George Poulos looked grim. It was a question he wouldn't mind knowing the answer to himself.

Nick sat propped up by giant pillows in the middle of Jodie's bed, strumming a beat-up old guitar he'd found in the corner. His skin glistened softly in the candlelight.

Jodie snuggled in close to his side. 'It's really nice, you know ... just the two of us.'

Nick dropped a kiss on the top of her head. 'Yeah,' he agreed. 'Is this your guitar, or your sister's?'

'It's mine,' said Jodie. 'Why?'

'You didn't tell me you knew how to play. Can you play something for me?'

Jodie shimmied up the bed until she was sitting up. 'Yeah, all right,' she said, taking the guitar from him.

She strummed a few chords, then began singing in a soft, broken voice.

Lying next to you
Like a child born into this world now
Shaking
Every moment here is like heaven
You feel it too
My heart's breaking

96

Over you . . .

She broke off for a moment, then started again.

And I will relate
Don't hesitate
I've fallen . . .
I'm lost in time
But just in time
For you . . .

She put down the guitar, and looked across at Nick, who was too stunned to speak for a moment. 'It's really beautiful,' he stammered, finally. 'Is that about me?'

Jodie nodded, smiling shyly. 'It's all I've written so far.'

Nick watched the shadows the flickering candles made on the wall for a moment. 'So you can really sing, eh?'

Jodie stiffened, letting the guitar slide to the floor. 'What's that supposed to mean?'

Nick squeezed her shoulder. 'It's not that I don't like your rap. I do. But hey – you can actually sing and play music. It's good.'

Jodie still felt a little miffed. 'So you don't think rap's music?'

'It's not what I meant,' said Nick, struggling to make himself clear. 'But if you can do both, why don't you? It'd be like me playing soccer but only using one leg.'

Jodie was silent for a moment. She'd never really considered performing anything publicly other than rap. Maybe some of those songs she'd been scribbling away at over the years had some commercial potential after all. It was something to think about, anyway.

But just for the moment, she had other things on her mind. And in her bed. 'Yeah, I guess you're right,' she said finally, reaching up and pulling Nick back down underneath the covers.

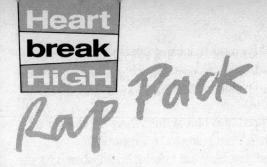

Chapter Eleven

Nick searched through his pockets for his door key, his chest heaving. He'd woken up when the morning sun had slanted through the blinds in Jodie's room, and realising just how much grief he was likely to face if his mother came into his room and found his bed empty, had run all the way home. He needn't have bothered. His dad was waiting in the hall for him anyway.

'Where the bloody hell have you been?' he screamed at Nick. 'Trini!' he called.

His mother appeared. 'We've been worried sick, Nicky,' she moaned, rushing over to him.

Nick tried to look cool. 'Hey, no need to worry, Ma. I stayed over at Con's – we were studying.' He headed into the kitchen. 'I know I should have called. But we just got so involved with our work. And then ...' The words died on his lips as he saw Con sitting at the kitchen table, a bowl of cornflakes in front of him. Oops.

Nick's father followed him into the kitchen, grabbing his arm. 'Now where the hell were you? And what were you doing all night? Stealing? Vandalising? Drinking? What?'

Nick shook off his father's hand. 'I was with Jodie, all right?'

'Jodie?' asked his mother, looking puzzled.

'My girlfriend,' said Nick simply. He turned to face his mother. 'Look, I'm sorry for worrying you, okay? Next time I'll call, I promise.'

His father ripped into him again. 'Where do you get off – "next time". There's not going to be a next time.'

Nick stormed past him and into his room, slamming the door behind him. 'Don't bet on it, Dad,' he muttered.

His father was furious. He ran to the door, banging his fist against it till it bruised. 'Nico! Nick!' he called. '*Anixe tin porta. Tora!*'

Mrs Poulos pulled away her husband's arm before he broke his hand. She led him into the loungeroom. 'That's enough, George.'

'While he's under my roof he will obey my rules,' muttered Mr Poulos, rubbing his knuckles.

His wife pursed her lips. 'You can't treat him like a child any more, George. He's eighteen ... a young man.'

Mr Poulos snorted. 'A man! Listen. A man understands his responsibilities. He respects his parents ... he doesn't stay out half the night without any thought for others.'

'George,' reasoned his wife, 'our Nico is growing up.' She sighed. 'We're going to lose him soon enough.' She slumped in her chair at the prospect, then straightened up as Nick appeared in the doorway.

'Look, Ma, I'm sorry, all right? I mean it.'

'Sorry isn't good enough,' she said, beckoning him into the room. 'You can't know what it's like until you've had a child of your own. Worrying that something might have happened to them ...'

Nick hung his head. 'It won't happen again, Ma.'

His father shot him a look. 'I just want to know why we haven't met this girl yet,' he asked softly.

'We've only been going out a short time,' explained Nick, eager to please now he was nearly off the hook.

His father looked shocked. 'Yet you're jumping into her bed together! *Mato Christos!*'

'Hey! We love each other!' said Nick. He turned to his mother. 'She's beautiful, she's smart – she's a nice person.'

Mrs Poulos smiled. 'So bring her home to dinner.'

'Yeah,' added her husband. 'I wanna meet this Wondergirl.'

Nick grinned. Things were getting back to normal again. 'I'll ask her today. At school,' he said, grabbing an apple from the fruitbowl and heading out into the street. 'Are you coming, Con?'

Jodie stood in front of the mirror, checking out the dress she was wearing. Maybe a little too over the top for conservative Greek parents, she wondered? It was black and figure-hugging, with a crocheted panel displaying her midriff. Way too over the top, she decided. Sighing, she pulled it off over her head, and padded into her sister's bedroom.

Linda had a lot of clothes, none of them to Jodie's taste. But they'd probably do the trick with Nick's Mum and Dad. She'd nearly died when he'd asked her to come to dinner at his house tonight. What was she supposed to say to his Mum: 'Thanks for your son – I really enjoyed sleeping with him last night'? Yeah, right.

She tried on a floral number. Spew! Then a little black dress. It made her look 35. Maybe a top and skirt? Not bad. She ran her fingers through her hair. Should she wear it up? – or down? In a topknot? Nothing looked right. She ripped everything off and started over . . .

Nick found his father sitting on the step out the back of the house. 'How's it going?' he asked tentatively, the morning's harsh words still ringing in his ears.

His father patted the step. 'Sit down, Nico.' He chose his words carefully. 'Your mother thinks I should have a bit of a chat with you.'

Nick looked embarrassed. 'What about?'

'Look, I'm sorry about this morning,' began his father. 'I was tired ... I was worried ...'

Nick stopped him. 'You don't have to explain. I was out of line.'

His father shook his head. 'I was out of line too. Nick, you're not a litttle boy any more. But parents always see the little boy, no matter how old you are.' He laughed suddenly, a faraway look in his eyes. 'Remember when we used to play soccer out here? You got a goal past me and you were only six. Remember what you said?'

Nick smiled at the memory. 'Suff-errr!!!'

His father laughed. 'I don't know. You grow up so fast. Your mother and I ... we worry about you because we love you and we want you to be happy.'

'I am happy,' said Nick. 'With Jodie.'

His father smiled and patted his knee. 'Good,' he said. 'You know, we're looking forward to meeting her tonight. I hope she likes Greek food, uh!'

'She will,' laughed Nick, getting up.

'Wait,' said his father, patting the step again. 'There's one more thing I want to ask you. Do you ... I mean ... how can I put this ...' He floundered for the right words. 'Being careful, you know?'

Nick laughed. Sometimes the old man was a real cracker.

'Relax, Dad,' he said, giving his father a gentle punch on the arm. 'We get heaps of sex education at school. In fact, if there's anything you want to know, just come and ask me, all right? I'll be inside.'

He pushed open the screen door, and headed for the kitchen. Mmmm. His mother was cooking up a storm. Everything was going to be okay.

Jodie was late. She'd panicked and run back home to change yet again, when she was only minutes away from the Poulos house. But George and Irini forgave her as soon as they realised what a treasure their son had brought home. She arrived bearing gifts for everyone – flowers for Irini, retsina for George, even chocolate for Effie.

Nick's mother had fussed around, getting her a drink, making her comfortable, admiring her clothes. His father told him twice how beautiful she was, and complimented him on his taste in women. Nick leaned back against the sideboard, drinking it all in. Sometimes – sometimes – families could be really nice things to belong to.

Chapter Twelve

I said get it down, play it out
Baby when you feel so raunchy ...

The music from Jodie's demo filtered around the music room. Brian hit rewind, then smiled across at Jodie. 'Well, that's it. The final mix. What do you think?'

Jodie's face was pale. She drummed her fingers on the desk. 'I don't know. Can't we put it down with more bass or something?'

'Look, Jodie. Don't stress, okay? It's fine. Anyway, you've got to take it to the guy this arvo.'

'It's great, Jodie,' Nick reassured her. 'He's going to love it.'

'Yeah, sure,' said Jodie, unconvinced. 'Do you know how many tapes these A&R guys listen to? Hundreds.'

'Not like yours, though,' said Nick, taking her hand.

Brian flipped the tape out of the player. 'Look, it's as good as we're going to get with this gear.'

Jodie looked at Nick. 'Will you come with me?'

Nick smiled. He'd been hanging out to be asked. 'Are you kidding? Of course I'll come with you.'

Jodie twined her arms around his neck and pulled his mouth towards hers. Brian watched them for a moment, then sighed. 'Hey you two,' he said, tapping Jodie on the shoulder, 'can you drop this other copy of the tape off to Mr Brown when you come up for air?'

Nick and Jodie clambered hand in hand up the steps of the record company office. 'Check out this place, will ya?' said Nick, impressed by the plush carpets and expensive wood panelling. 'Look at all those gold records and awards and stuff,' he said, pointing to display cases that lined the walls.' He squeezed Jodie's hand. 'One day, you're going to have your own record up there. Just you wait.'

'Yeah, sure,' said Jodie, too nervous to take much in. The receptionist sent them up to the top floor to meet with Max, the artist and repertoire guy. She prayed he was going to like her tape. He just *had* to.

'This looks like the place,' said Nick, stopping at a heavy wooden door with a brass nameplate. He knocked. The door was opened by a young guy in jeans, his crinkly hair pulled back in a ponytail. He shook Nick's hand.

'Max Furlong. Hi.' He turned to Jodie. 'How you doing, Jodie? Great to see you again. Did you bring your tape for me?'

Jodie nodded dumbly and handed it to him. This was it. Make or break time.

Max dropped the tape into a slot and hit play. Nick's eyebrows shot up. Wow! It sounded a hundred per cent better through this guy's system. Maybe Jodie had a chance after all!

Jodie sat on the edge of her seat, too scared to check Max's face for a reaction. When the tape stopped, she held her breath.

It seemed to take for ever for Max to speak. 'Yep ... there's something interesting there,' he said finally. 'It's raw ... but I like it.' He flipped the tape out of the player and snapped it into its case. 'Look, let me try it on some other people, okay? I'll get back to you by the end of the week.'

Jodie's eyes shone. 'You really like it?' she asked, stunned.

Max smiled. He scooped up an envelope from a pile on the desk and handed it to Jodie. 'Look, I'm not going to jerk you around, okay? I haven't got the time.' He moved across to the door, opening it for them. 'It's been good to meet you. Enjoy the show.'

Nick pushed a bewildered Jodie out into the hallway. 'Hey, cool,' he said. 'He went for it!'

Jodie was walking on air, trying to come to terms with what had happened. 'Huh?' she said vaguely.

'So what's in the envelope?' asked Nick, grabbing it from her and ripping it open. 'Oh, wow!'

'What is it?' asked Jodie, stumbling on the thick carpet.

'Tickets! The Baby Animals. For tomorrow night.' He waved another pile of coupons. 'And look! Backstage passes. Man, that guy must have loved you!'

'Yeah,' said Jodie, finally reaching the street door. She pushed it open, a smile splitting her face. 'He must have! So what will we do? Celebrate? Let's go back to my place. We can get some drinks ... '

Nick checked his watch. 'Oh man, no!' he cried, slapping his forehead.

Jodie looked alarmed. 'What's up?'

'It's nearly six o'clock! It'll take ages to get home from the city.'

'So?'

'So I promised Dad I'd be home by six every night this week. He freaked out at Parent Teacher Night the other night. Ms Milano told him I wasn't doing enough work. So now, I've gotta be home every night in my room – studying.'

'*Every* night?' asked Jodie. She tapped the tickets. 'What about these? The concert's tomorrow night. Look, there's ... there's eight tickets here. We can give them out to Con and Rose and everyone. Make a night of it.'

Nick looked glum. 'There's no way he's going to let me go.' He kicked moodily at a pebble on the footpath. 'He'll probably ground me for coming home late tonight as it is. You don't know him.'

Jodie smiled. 'So? Talk to him. It's only one night, isn't it? Tell him you'll do double homework the next night.'

Nick shook his head slowly, remembering his father's face when he'd come in that night from Jodie's place. He was like a rock when he'd made up his mind about something. Unbudgeable.

Jodie wrinkled her nose. 'You're not going to do it, are you,' she said, her dreams of a big night of celebrating with Nick seeping away.

Nick crumpled the envelope the tickets had been in, flicking it into the gutter. 'There's no point. I either ignore him, or I do what he says.'

Jodie picked out their bus, trundling through the peak hour traffic towards them. 'It's a pity,' she threw back over her shoulder, heading over to the bus stop. 'It's going to be a *great* night.'

Jodie swept into Ruby's, dressed to the max. Tight red dress, platform shoes, chunky silver jewellery. Her hair, piled high on her head, and her heavy makeup made her look like a fashion model.

Con and Steve stopped their game of pool and turned to stare. 'Woooo!' said Con. 'We've got a girl at school who looks a bit like you. Her name's Jodie.'

Jodie grinned. 'Like your shoes, Steve,' she said, admiring his red lace-up Docs.

'Are you kidding?' said Danielle. 'They're gross. He just better not stand next to me.' She turned to Con, who was flashing an autograph book around. 'What's that for? You can't go round collecting autographs.'

'Why not?' asked Con seriously. 'There's a big market for celebrity autographs.'

Danielle shook her head. 'You're an embarrassment, Con.'

Jodie gasped as a pair of hands slid round her waist. 'Nick!' she cried. She turned to kiss him hello. 'Hey! I thought you weren't coming.'

'And miss this dress?' said Nick. 'You look hot.'

'Thanks,' said Jodie. 'So do you.' She lowered her voice. 'How did it go with your Dad?'

'It's cool,' said Nick, kissing her neck. He wasn't about to tell her that the whole thing was totally uncool. He'd been right about his father grounding him for coming in late last night. His Dad had been sitting waiting for him in the hallway, ready to jump on him the minute he crept in the front door. He'd gone on and on at him again about the importance of doing well at school and getting a good job. Nick had tried to tell him about the concert but it had only made things worse. Much worse. He wished he'd never agreed to the stupid six o'clock rule in the first place.

It was all really unfair. Surely he had some say in how he

organised his own life? Well, his father couldn't push him around for ever. Things were going to change – starting tonight.

He kissed Jodie again. 'So what are we waiting for? The band'll be starting without us. Let's go!'

It was after one when Nick finally made it home. After the concert they'd all gone to a cafe in the Cross, then shared taxis back to Hartley. Nick closed the front door quietly, then, taking off his shoes, crept down the hallway towards his room. Made it, he thought, his hand on the door-handle.

A light clicked on. His father, still in his work-clothes, stood framed in the doorway of the living room.

His voice was cold. 'We had an agreement ... you made me a promise ... and the first night, you break it.'

'But, Dad, tonight was really special ... '

'I don't care what you were doing,' his father snapped. 'We had an agreement.'

'Oh, come on, Dad,' pleaded Nick. Why was he being such a pain about this? It was only one o'clock. He knew plenty of kids whose fathers couldn't care if they'd come in at all!

'You don't break promises in this house,' continued Mr Poulos. 'Not to me. I'm your father!'

Nick started to take off his jacket. He could see there was no way he was going to get out of this one. Not once his father started on his 'family responsibilities' thing.

Nick's father waved a piece of paper in his face. 'Now I find you haven't been going to school! I got a letter today, from the government. "Please explain why your son has missed school on three separate occasions." What do I say to that? Very sorry, but my son's got a girlfriend?'

Nick shrugged uneasily. 'Say what you like.'

'I'll say what I said before!' shouted his father. 'You come home straight after school. You don't go anywhere. And you stop seeing Jodie through the week!'

'Ah, c'mon,' pleaded Nick, desperately. 'Listen to me, would you?' But his father was not to be swayed.

'No! You listen! You can see her on the weekends.' He paused for breath, then began again, more slowly. 'As long as you live here, you do what I say.' He folded his arms – finished with the matter.

Nick slammed into his bedroom. 'Fine!' he shouted back over his shoulder. 'If that's the way you want it ...'

'Nick ...' Mr Poulos followed his son into the room, where he found him stashing T-shirts and jeans into his kit bag. He tried to grab the bag from him. 'Now what are you doing? Come on, stop that.'

Nick pushed his hand away. 'No, you're absolutely right, Dad. This is your house. If I leave, we won't have anything to argue about, will we?' He upturned his sock drawer onto the bed and began stuffing socks and jocks into his bag.

His father sighed. 'Do you think it's easy out there?' he asked. 'How are you going to live, eh?'

Nick kept packing, his head down. 'Well, that's my problem, all right? Don't you worry about it.'

His father moved over to the bookcase, where Nick kept his soccer trophies. He picked one up, rolling it around in his hands. 'Look, Nico,' he began, his voice shaky. 'Please ... don't do this. Just ... don't ...' His voice trailed off.

Nick grabbed the trophy from him and threw it into the bag beside his soccer jumper. 'Nobody ... *nobody* ... tells me how to run my life. All right?'

'All right,' said his father. 'But what about Jodie, eh? I mean,

I'm only trying to give you a chance in this world.'

'I've already got a chance!' said Nick indignantly, zipping up his bag and moving towards the door.

His father watched him leave. 'All right ... get out ... go, okay!' he screamed, following Nick out into the hall. He winced as the front door slammed in his face, then trundled sadly into his bedroom.

Jodie woke to the sound of someone hammering on her front door. Slipping on her kimono, she padded sleepily out to the loungeroom. 'Who is it?' she asked, stifling a yawn.

'It's me, okay?' said Nick. 'Can you let me in?'

Jodie unhooked the chain and opened the door. Nick stepped in quickly and hugged her. By the look on his face, she decided, something pretty bad had gone down. She kissed him, then snuggled into his chest. 'What's up?' she asked.

Nick sighed. 'I came here because ... you're the only one who won't tell me to go home.' He searched her face for an answer. 'Will you?'

Jodie pulled away. This was major stuff. Spending the odd night with Nick was one thing. She wasn't sure she wanted to take him on permanently just yet. 'My sister will be back on the weekend,' she reminded him.

Nick kissed her neck. 'Just for a couple of days?' he pleaded.

Poor bastard, thought Jodie. If he has had a full-on row with this father, he's probably going to need a fair dose of TLC. She relented. 'Sure,' she said, her arms moving around his waist.

Nick looked down at her. He gently brushed a spare wisp of hair out of her eyes. 'Thanks,' he said, before launching into a long, sweet kiss.

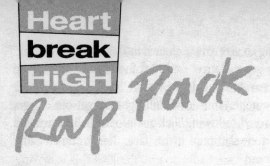

Chapter Thirteen

'Nick!' called Jodie. 'Have you finished in the bathroom yet? I'm late as it is.'

Nick, a towel wrapped round his waist, opened the bathroom door. Columns of steam escaped. 'Slow down,' he said, kissing her. 'I was just going to make breakfast for us.'

Jodie pushed him away. 'Come on, Nick. I have to go to school.'

'Why?' asked Nick, opening the fridge and extracting a carton of eggs.

'To see Brian,' said Jodie. 'Aren't you going in?'

Nick cracked an egg into a frying pan. 'Maybe later,' he said, blowing her a kiss.

Jodie stared at him. 'Nick... you're not thinking of dropping out, are you?'

Nick filled the kettle. 'Hey, I can't stay on. I've left home, I need money ... I've got to get a job.'

'Nick, think about what you're saying.'

'What?' He flipped the eggs over, wincing as the hot fat spattered his arm.

'Slow down, that's all,' said Jodie, taking a step towards him.

'Look, think about it. Leaving your family is one thing – but school too?'

'Who said I've left my family?' said Nick, surprised and angered by Jodie's line of questioning. 'I'm setting up a new home so I need a job.' He flipped the eggs again and turned off the gas. 'It's simple.'

Jodie's eyes widened. 'How do you think all this is making me feel?' she asked.

The kettle boiled. Nick reached over and flicked the switch. 'You don't have to feel anything,' he said flatly. 'It's got nothing to do with you.'

Jodie stared at him, appalled. Grabbing her bag from the kitchen table, she slammed out of the room. Nick looked down unhappily at the congealing eggs. 'I didn't mean that ... ' he whispered, his shoulders slumping.

Jodie was bowled over in the school corridor by an enthusiastic Steve and Danielle. 'Jodie, you legend!' cried Steve, picking her up and swinging her around. 'That concert was fantastic.'

'Wicked,' agreed Danielle. 'Wasn't it, Chaka?'

'Unreal,' she agreed. She glanced down the corridor. 'Where's Nick?'

'Umm ... ' began Jodie, moving towards her locker.

Con blocked her way. 'Yeah,' he said, his face dark. 'Where is Nick?'

Jodie turned the key. 'I don't know,' she shrugged, trying to look vague.

Con's hand whipped out to grab Jodie's arm, spinning her round to face him. 'Look, I was around his place this morning. Like I usually am. His parents reckon there was a blue last night. He didn't stay with you by any chance, did he?'

113

Jodie shrugged again. Danielle picked up on what was going down. 'Woooo! He's moved in? That is so romantic,' she crooned, sarcastically.

'Take it easy, Danni,' jumped in Chaka.

'Why?' asked Danielle. 'What's wrong with that?'

Steve scratched his head. 'We talking major problem here, Jodie?' he asked.

Jodie's face was mutinous. 'I don't know, why are you asking me?'

'Because he's living with you!' said Con.

Jodie held up her hands. 'Look, he came round and I did what any of you would have done if he'd turned up on your doorstep. I let him stay.' She glared at Con. 'What's bugging you, Con, anyway? That he didn't turn up at your house?'

'Geez, Jodie,' appealed Rose, 'we're worrying about a mate!'

Jodie backed down a tad. 'Yeah?' she said softly. 'Well, so am I. He's quit school, he's out looking for work.' Having found the books she needed, she closed her locker and moved off down the corridor.

Con was the first to react. 'He's quit school?' he called after her.

Jodie stopped and turned around. 'You heard me!' she said angrily, before heading into Room 27.

Con took the steps of the railway bridge two at a time. He could see Nick down the street a bit, coming out of the CES, a look of gloom on his face. He hurried to catch him up.

'What's wrong with you, mate?' yelled Con, pulling at Nick's shirt. 'You quit school and you leave home!'

Nick shrugged him off. 'Look, I don't want to talk about it.'

'You never want to talk!'

114

'Ah, you don't know anything about it,' said Nick, moving off down the street.

Con blocked his way. 'So you tell me, uh? You get the hots for Jodie and you move into her flat ... share it together. Live happily ever after. Is that it?'

'Just shut up!' said Nick, trying to move past him.

'No, I won't,' screamed Con, forcing Nick to look at him. 'What's wrong, man ... use your brain.' His voice softened. 'You're my cousin, man ... I care about you. I'm not going to just sit around and see you wreck your life.'

Nick jabbed a finger in Con's face. 'Hey, I'm not wrecking anything. I'm sick of getting nowhere at school and I'm sick of living at home!'

'So what's new?' asked Con. 'You don't leave home because of one argument.'

'This is different, all right? I want to be with Jodie.'

'Oh right. This is your idea, is it?'

Nick stared at him. What was he up to? 'We both want it,' he said flatly.

'You sure about that? Uh? She didn't seem too happy about it this morning.'

'Crap!' sneered Nick.

'And what are you gonna live on?' jeered Con. 'Cat food?'

'I'm gonna get a job,' said Nick. 'Don't worry, I'll find one. I've got plans.'

Con laughed. 'Get real! Who's gonna hire you? You can't do anything but kick a soccer ball.'

Nick had had enough. He pushed past Con, heading further up the street. 'I can look after myself!' he called back.

Con watched his disappearing back with increasing despair. *Scata*, he thought. Now what was he going to do?

Jodie looked up as Nick came into the flat, hauling plastic shopping bags. 'So where've you been?' she asked.

Nick sighed. 'I told you – I was out looking for work.'

Jodie pointed to the bags. 'What doing? Home deliveries?'

Nick dropped the bags onto the bench. 'What's wrong with you?'

'I'm copping the blame for you leaving school.'

Nick sighed. He hadn't wanted things to work out like this.

'Have you talked to your parents?' Jodie asked him.

'I'll talk to them, okay?'

'When, tomorrow?'

Nick grinned. 'Yeah, big day tomorrow.'

'Why?'

Nick blew her a kiss. 'Your mate at the record company's secretary rang. You've got an appointment at three tomorrow.'

'You're kidding!' Jodie gasped. 'What else did he say?'

'That's it,' said Nick, fossicking through the bags. 'I bought some things to celebrate. Chicken breasts, tomatoes, pasta. I'll even cook!'

Jodie's face softened. She moved over to him. 'Oh, Nick,' she sighed, twining her arms round his neck. 'Things are going to work out for us, you'll see.'

'You bet they will,' said Nick, holding her close. 'Today, Hartley – tomorrow, the world. London, L.A. – so long as we're together, we can do anything I reckon.' He pulled away, and began unpacking the rest of the bag.

Jodie watched him slicing up tomatoes. Tomorrow the world, eh? It sounded great. She just wished she could share Nick's optimism one hundred per cent.

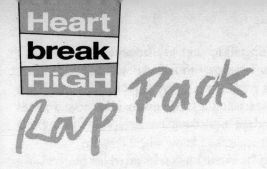

Chapter Fourteen

Mr Poulos stood at the kitchen door. His daughter, Effie, was sitting up at the table, concentrating on her homework. His wife was at the sink, chopping vegetables for dinner. Neither of them was smiling.

Usually when he came home from work, everyone was laughing and happy. Effie would climb up onto his knee and tell him everything that had happened at school. Irini would give him a kiss and ask him how his day had gone. Today there was just gloom. Nick was still gone.

Hearing footsteps, Mrs Poulos looked around hopefully. 'I haven't heard anything from him yet,' she said, when she saw it was only her husband.

'Neither have I. What am I supposed to do?'

Mrs Poulos put down her knife. 'For a start, forget that you're angry with him. Just remember that you love him.'

Mr Poulos nodded. 'I'm not angry. Not really. I'm afraid for Nick ... afraid that he will leave school, get a job and spend his whole life hating it.'

'Is that what you do?'

Mr Poulos sighed. 'I don't hate my life, but my job could

117

be better. Who wants to work in a factory all their life?'

Mrs Poulos moved over to him. 'Look, it's not like it was when we were growing up. Everything is so much freer these days – less restricted. If a father makes rules now, a son is going to go out and break them. For me, it's enough to know that my kids are safe and I know where they are.'

'How do you know that's he's safe?' asked her husband. 'We don't know anything about this girl. They could be ...'

'Do you really think that? Jodie goes to school, has her own place to live. It's not like our son has taken up with some street kid who lives in a dump bin or hangs out down in the Cross. Nick's not stupid, you know!'

Her husband sat down at the table, his head in his hands. 'So I should do nothing?'

Mrs Poulos massaged his shoulders. 'Just try to understand him, eh?'

Jodie sat across the desk from Max Furlong, her heart thumping double-time. *Pleeeeease let him have liked it*, she thought.

He pushed the cassette across the desktop to her. 'Thanks for that, Jodie. It was, ah, great.'

Jodie's lip trembled. 'You don't want it,' she blurted. She reached automatically for her bag, and tried to stand up.

Max smiled. 'Hang on a minute, Jodie. The other guys like your sound as much as I do.'

'But ...'

'You're just not ready yet.' He settled back in his chair, arms behind his head. 'See, it takes a lot of money to launch an act. We need to be sure. What we would like to do is put you with a band. Now, they're really good, they're on contract to us ... but they need something extra.'

Jodie looked up at him, stunned, 'Me?'

Max smiled again. 'They need your voice.'

Jodie beamed. They liked her voice. She actually had a chance of making it in the music world! 'So what kind of line-up is it?' she asked excitedly.

'Ah, two guitars, drums, bass ... possibly a keyboard.'

'A rock band,' said Jodie, just managing to keep the disappointment out of her voice. It wasn't really what she'd been aiming for. Still ...

Max's eyes twinkled. 'Yeah, I know – it's a rock band. But hey – it will be good experience for you.'

Jodie nodded. He was right. 'So when do I meet them?'

'When can you go?'

'Where?' asked Jodie, alarm bells screaming in her head.

Max's face was impassive. 'Melbourne.'

Back in her flat, Jodie made herself a cup of lemon tea and lay back on the sofa, quietly freaking out. Melbourne? They wanted her to go to Melbourne? Moving didn't bother her – she'd done enough of that in her life. But it would mean leaving Nick ... unless he decided to come with her. Maybe that would be the answer to both their problems. Seeing as he'd already made the big break and left home anyway ...

Her thoughts were interrupted by a polite tap on the door. Putting down her mug, she hurried over to open it.

'Oh ... hello, Mrs Poulos.' Jodie's face burned. 'Ah ... Nick isn't here, I'm afraid.'

Mrs Poulos looked past her, into the flat. 'But he's staying here?'

'Yes.'

'Good,' said Mrs Poulos, breaking into a smile. 'Better than

119

in the street or somewhere terrible.' She leaned towards Jodie. 'I think it's good that Nick is not here, uh? Maybe you and me can have a talk?'

Jodie shrugged. 'Sure,' she said, inviting Nick's mother into the flat. 'Would you like a cup of tea? I've just made some.'

'That would be lovely,' said Mrs Poulos, settling down on the sofa. 'Nick tells me you're making a career as a singer?'

Jodie handed her the tea and sat down opposite her. 'I'm hoping to.'

Mrs Poulos stirred her tea thoughtfully. 'Very hard.'

'I know,' said Jodie, staring at the cushions, her fingers twisting their fringed ends. 'Mrs Poulos,' she blurted out, finally, 'I've been offered a great opportunity.'

'Take it.'

'Sorry?' asked Jodie, surprised at the older woman's directness.

'Take it. You've been given a chance, you have to take it. So, tell me about it.'

Jodie grinned shyly. 'This record company wants me to join a band in Melbourne. Nick ... ah, Nick doesn't know yet.'

Mrs Poulos sighed and sipped her tea. 'And do you want him to come with you?'

'I love him,' said Jodie simply.

Mrs Poulos smiled. 'Yes, I can see that, and I can see that Nick loves you. But whether it's a one-day love or a lifetime love ... I don't know.' She sighed. 'There's all sorts of love.'

Jodie dug her fingers deeper into the cushion. 'I don't know anyone in Melbourne.'

'But you will make friends! You've got the band – it will be a whole new world.' She put down her cup. 'What about Nick? He will have no one.'

'He makes friends easily,' pointed out Jodie.

'True. So you will tell Nick and let him decide?'

Jodie nodded glumly.

'But he won't decide. Not really. If you tell Nick he'll drop everything and come with you. He won't even think about it.'

Jodie sighed. Nick's mother was making a lot of sense. She wished her own mother could have been so understanding when she'd had problems. But it didn't change the fact that there was still a hard decision to make. 'What should I do?'

'You have to decide.'

'Well, I know what I want,' said Jodie firmly. 'I want to go to Melbourne.'

Mrs Poulos sighed. 'You have to decide about Nick. He won't even stop to think about it.' She picked up her cup again. 'You know, I was about the same age as Nick when I left home. I got married . . . I came to live in Australia. I left all my family and my friends behind. It was very hard, you know? And that was for love.' She took a long sip, then looked at Jodie. 'Tell me, Jodie, if Nick asked you to go and live in Greece with him, back to our village – give up your music career – would you do it?'

Jodie stared at the table. Even *she* didn't know the answer to that one. Nick's mother was making this all too hard. 'But I can't just vanish and not tell Nick what's happening,' she said, finally.

'No,' agreed his mother. 'Either you ask him – and he will say yes, believe me – or you tell him there's no room.'

Jodie was appalled at the suggestion. 'But I love him.'

Mrs Poulos smiled. 'I know. That's what makes it so hard.' She stood up, ready to leave. 'My son has found himself a nice girl.'

Jodie was torn. 'What should I do?' she asked.

121

'What you feel is right,' said Mrs Poulos, moving across to the door. 'I'll show myself out.'

Jodie burst into Ruby's looking for Nick. She found him at the back pool table, moodily potting balls. 'What's wrong?' she asked. 'Why didn't you come home?'

Nick slammed a ball into a pocket. 'I don't know. Everything's just getting too much.'

'Like what?' asked Jodie.

'The other kids, you know? Con. Rose. They're all giving me a hard time. Telling me I'm stupid for moving in with you.'

'Yeah, I know,' said Jodie, picking up a ball and spinning it. 'I'm copping it too, don't you worry. They're trying to say it's my fault that you left home.' She bowled the ball along the table, hitting the black. 'Well, you won't have to worry about them any more, all right? It's not going to be an issue any more.'

Nick stared at her. 'What do you mean?'

Jodie looked down at the table. 'The record company offered me work,' she said quietly.

'That's great!'

'It's with a band. In Melbourne.'

Nick raced round the table and hugged her. 'Even better! We can get away from all the bitching and crap and make a fresh start ...' He broke off, feeling Jodie stiffen. Something was wrong.

'I have to go ... immediately ...'

'What's all this "I have to go" business?' His voice grew louder. 'You mean, I'm not invited? Is that what you're saying?'

'Nick, I'm going to be really tied up with the band.'

'Doesn't leave much over for me, does it?' said Nick angrily.

'You have your own life to lead ... here,' pleaded Jodie.

Nick grabbed her hands. 'But I want to be with you!'

Jodie pulled away. 'Doing what, Nick? Carrying my bags, waiting for me to get back from gigs? You'll probably end up getting some dead-end job. What about your friends? Your family?'

'So what? I'd have you, wouldn't I?'

'How long for?'

Nick was stunned. This couldn't be Jodie talking to him. She'd told him she loved him!

'Thanks a lot, Jodie. I should have expected this. As soon as you get a shot at being rich and famous you turn around and dump me. So all that love stuff you said was just crap, uh?'

Jodie hung her head. 'There's all different kinds of love,' she said, echoing his mother's words.

'Yeah, sure,' said Nick, turning away.

Jodie grabbed his arm, spinning him round to face her. 'It's true, all right?' she said. 'It's why I don't want you to come to Melbourne with me.'

Nick shrugged her off. 'Just get out of my face,' he spat, slamming his way out of the cafe.

Con, who'd been watching the exchange with concern, caught up with Nick in the street. 'Hey, mate, slow down, wouldya? What's the problem?' He sat down on a bench, pulling Nick down beside him.

'Jodie's hit the big time,' said Nick. 'Hooked up with some band down in Melbourne.'

'So ... what's the problem?'

'She doesn't want me to go,' said Nick. 'Reckons I'd get in the way.' He hung his head. 'Did she make a fool of me, or what?'

'No way, mate,' Con reassured him. 'Jodie wouldn't con you.

123

She loves you! Anybody can see that. There's got to be some other reason she's doing this.'

'Yeah,' said Nick. 'She'll be too busy mixing with "important" music types.'

Con shook his head. 'Geez, mate, you can be so blind sometimes. I think she's done the right thing, you know? Telling you that? And you know what else? I bet it must have hurt.'

'It does.'

Con slapped his forehead. 'Hurt *her*, not you, dickbrain. Stop feeling sorry for yourself and think about her! What if she did want you to go? And what if she could see there's nothing for you in Melbourne except watching her drift away? She did it for *you*, mate!'

Nick stared at him, a slow smile creeping over his face. 'Yeah,' he whispered. 'Yeah! You may be right!'

Jodie transferred the messy pile of clothes from her bed to her suitcase. This hadn't been the way she'd wanted to leave town, slipping away with everyone down on her. She should have been out partying, celebrating her new career. That would just have to wait till Melbourne, now. She threw her sexy red dress on top of the pile.

'That's gonna get crushed,' said a voice behind her.

Jodie spun round. It was Nick, holding out a rose. She took it from him, her eyes filling.

'Hey, it's only plastic,' said Nick, stroking her cheek. 'Best I could do at this time of night. I'm sorry, Jodie.'

She moved into his arms and waggled her head against his chest. 'The timing's lousy, that's all.'

Nick sighed. 'So when do you go?'

'Tomorrow morning – on the plane. I . . . I'll try and drop in to school on the way. Say goodbye.'

'The guys will never forgive you if you don't.'

Jodie kissed his chest. 'I wish we had more time.'

'Tell me about it,' laughed Nick. 'Still . . . the worst thing would be if we ended up hating each other. That'd be even worse than saying goodbye like this.'

'I'm really going to miss you, Nick.'

'I'm gonna miss you too,' said Nick, kissing her. 'You know, when you're really famous and stuff I'm going to be at every show. And I wanna be in the front row, okay?'

Jodie grinned at him through her tears. 'Are you kidding? You'll be backstage in the VIP room with me.'

Nick walked into the Poulos dining room just as his family were beginning their evening meal. His mother jumped up. 'Sit,' she said, hiding a grin, 'your dinner's in the oven.' She moved out into the kitchen.

Nick looked at his father for a cue. Mr Poulos kept shovelling spanakopita into his mouth, his eyes averted. Nick sat down, anyway. He'd get through to him somehow.

He smiled at Effie. 'How did she know to keep my dinner hot tonight?' he asked, incredulously.

Effie grinned conspiratorially. 'She didn't. She keeps it every night!' She put down her fork. 'Are you staying?'

Nick looked across at his father. Still no sign of recognition from him that he'd come back to the house. 'Yep,' he said, brightly.

Effie smiled, and picked up her fork again. 'That's good.'

'Nick!' called his mother from the kitchen. 'Can I see you for a moment?'

Nick stumbled to his feet. A hand grasped his arm. His father, his voice shaky with emotion, finally spoke. 'Nick. Nicos. This is your home, okay? As much as it is mine.' He stood up, embracing his son. 'I can't stop you leaving ... but remember, the door is always open.'

Nick hugged his father. Mrs Poulos, watching from the kitchen, threw a quick smile at Effie. Everything was okay. Her family was home, together again.

The bell rang. The kids trundled out into the corridor, glad to be finished with first period. Con gave Nick a push. 'Man, that Social Studies teacher is so boring. Do you reckon we could arrange an early retirement for him, or what?'

'Yeah,' said Nick gloomily, checking his watch. He peered up and down the busy corridor, searching for a familiar blonde head.

'So where's Jodie?' asked Con, opening his locker.

'Yeah,' added Rose. 'Where is Jodie?'

'Dunno. She said she'd be here.'

'Probably chickened out,' said Danielle.

'I'm not surprised after what you guys said to her,' shot back Con.

'Aw, lay off it,' said Rose. 'You didn't exactly kiss her feet.'

Chaka juggled her books, searching for her locker key. 'We were all pretty mean, hey. But I thought she would say goodbye at least.'

Rivers stuck his shaggy head in Nick's face. 'Yeah, well, good riddance, I say.'

Nick slammed his locker shut. 'No one asked you!'

'Ooooo, what's the matter, lover boy?' whined Rivers, out for a chance to stir. 'A bit touchy since you've been dumped?'

Nick's fingers curled into a fist. 'Shut your mouth or I'll shut it for you!' he yelled.

Rivers tapped two fingers on Nick's chest. 'Any time, loser,' he sneered.

Con glanced at Steve, who nodded. 'Okay, break it up, you two!' yelled Steve, stepping in and pushing Rivers out of the way, while Con hauled Nick to the side.

'Hey!' called Chaka. 'Look, there she is!'

Nick stared. Jodie was floating down the corridor towards him, looking sensational in crochet and flares. His heart stopped.

Danielle dropped her bag, and ran to hug Jodie. 'Hey!' she cried. 'We didn't think you'd show!'

Jodie looked past her to Nick. Why wasn't he coming over? 'Yeah, well I'm not really good at goodbyes and stuff,' she explained.

Danielle kissed her. 'Well, anyway, good luck.'

'Yeah,' added Steve, 'I wish we could have a couple of drinks to celebrate your success or something. Waddya reckon?'

Jodie smiled, touched by their generosity. 'Yeah, I'd love to, but my cab's waiting ...'

'That's okay,' said Rose, 'we just wanted to wish you luck.'

'Yeah, good luck, hey,' said Jack, kissing her shyly. 'You'll do great.'

One by one the group filtered away, off to their next class. Only Nick was left. He took Jodie's hand and walked slowly out to the street with her. 'Well, I guess this is it, then,' he said, too scared of what he might see to look into her eyes.

'Yeah, I guess so.' She pulled him towards her, kissing his neck, then his mouth.

'Jodie . . .' began Nick, then changed his mind. He returned the kiss. A horn blared. Jodie ignored it for as long as she could, then finally pulled away.

'Look, I gotta go, okay . . .?' She shoved a folded piece of paper into his hand.

Nick nodded dumbly. He walked her over to the cab in a daze, opening the back door for her.

The cab pulled out into the traffic, Jodie's face at the window. Nick watched it disappear round the corner, and out of his life. Maybe forever. Who knew?

He sat down in the gutter, too shell-shocked to go back into school. Heartbreak High, they called it. Yeah, well, maybe they were right.

He stared at the piece of paper in his hand. Jodie's new address in Melbourne, he supposed. He unfolded it slowly. Inside, written in neat, curvy handwriting, were the words to a song. His song. The song Jodie had written – just for him.

And I will relate
Don't hesitate
I've fallen . . .
I'm lost in time
But just in time
For you . . .

Jodie . . . how would he ever live without her?

DODGEM

Bernard Ashley

Cooped up in council care, Simon and Rose plan a daring escape.

Life hasn't been easy for Simon Leighton. Since the death of his mother, he has had to cope with a depressed father. Afraid to leave him on his own for too long, Simon plays truant from school to look after him. But this eventually lands Simon in council care and his father in hospital.

In the home, Simon develops a grudging relationship with a tough young girl called Rose and together they hatch a daring scheme which takes them on an escape route through run-down city streets to the noisy, bustling world of the fairground.

BASKETBALL GAME

Julius Lester

Allen likes girls, but he mustn't be seen with this one.

Allen is black and Rebecca is white, and in Nashville, Tennessee, in 1956 that means they must keep apart. They like each other, they're interested in each other, but is that enough to survive the deeply rooted prejudice that surrounds them?

BY LEXIE ROBERTS
Kerry Kenihan

From the floor, she picked up the unfinished *Sweet Semester*. At least here she would find a happy ending.

Lexie's family is going broke. Her parents have enough problems of their own, and leave Lexie to manage the chaotic household, her hyperactive brother and somehow prepare for her final year – twelve exams. Even her relationship with Michael is fraught with difficulties.

Her only escape is the fantasy world of romantic novels. Gradually, secretly, late at night, she is inspired to crystallize her hopes for the future and begins to write her own Teendream . . .

FACING UP
Robin F. Brancato

How do you face up to the worst mistake of your life?

Dave and Jep are the closest of friends. They are opposites in character but that makes life more interesting, and Dave doesn't even mind Jep's girlfriend Susan tagging along. But things change when Susan makes a play for Dave. Torn between Jep's friendship and Susan's love, Dave feels sickened, but before he can explain to his friend, a tragic accident changes everything, for ever.

MADAME DOUBTFIRE

Anne Fine

A vast apparition towered over her on the doorstep. It wore a loose salmon pink coat . . . and tucked under its arm was an enormous imitation crocodile skin handbag . . . 'I'm Madame Doubtfire, dear.'

Lydia, Christopher and Natalie Hilliard are used to domestic turmoil and have been torn between their warring parents ever since the divorce. But all that changes when their mother takes on a most unusual cleaning lady. Despite her extraordinary appearance, Madame Doubtfire turns out to be a talented and efficient housekeeper and, for a short time at least, the arrangement is a resounding success. But, as the Hilliard children soon discover, there's more to Madame Doubtfire than domestic talents . . .

SWEET FRANNIE

Susan Sallis

Fran desperately wants to be treated like an ordinary teenager.

Paralysed from the waist down and confined to a wheelchair, Fran realizes she hasn't much of a future, but when she goes into Thornton Hall Residential Home, things begin to look up. For a start, she has a room of her own for the first time in her life. And pretty soon there's someone else to think about: eighteen-year-old Luke Hawkins. After all, who better than fiercely independent Fran to help a young boy who has just lost both his legs in a road accident?